THE LOST PRINCE

OF CARBENIA

THE LOST PRINCE

OF CARBENIA

BY CAROLINE R EDRALIN

SMART NURSING SOLUTION AGENCY, LLC

COLUMBUS, OH

ACKNOWLEDGMENTS

A moment comes in a person's life when he dares explore beyond the limits of his comfort zone. Then the realization dawns that there are talents left undiscovered when limits are imposed on oneself without probing the possibilities of the unknown.

Writing a book is a talent. It takes a special person to create a story based on one's imagination and creative thinking.

I would like to thank the Lord for bringing out this talent in me that I did not know I possess. I also would like to acknowledge the contributions of the following people. They have unselfishly given their time, efforts and commitment to make this project become a reality.

Geraldine E Baggs –Thank you for patiently editing this manuscript.

Erben Detablan, Animator/Illustrator– Thank you for providing the art illustrations and the book cover for this book.

Mary Ramirez – Thank you, Mom, for supporting this dream. You have given me the "boost" that I needed to keep working on this book.

Catherine E Rebuldela – Thank you for always willingly lending a helping hand and for lending a listening ear as well.

Mary Ann Joy Lee-Royeca – Thank you for assisting with some computer-related tasks to help put this book together.

You are all God's blessing to me. Thank you for being a part of my life.

TABLE OF CONTENTS

INTRODUCTION... 2

CHAPTER 1   The weird dream...4

CHAPTER 2   Fantasy that coincides with reality............ 9

CHAPTER 3   Meeting the mysterious neighbor.............15

CHAPTER 4   The encounter with the woman of his

dreams.. 21

CHAPTER 5   Compromising photos of "The Prince".....25

CHAPTER 6   More crime fighting dreams...................... 29

CHAPTER 7   The date..34

CHAPTER 8   Attack at the park.......................................38

CHAPTER 9   Damon Yucca, the evil warrior................. 42

CHAPTER 10   Cain, the first murderer in the history of

mankind.. 51

CHAPTER 11   The initial confrontation between Richard

Blake and Damon Yucca........................... 55

CHAPTER 12   The man in the shadows........................ 58

CHAPTER 13   The plan for a massive destruction.......... 63

CHAPTER 14   The revelation................................... 67

CHAPTER 15   The reunion...................................... 80

CHAPTER 16   The Kingdom of Carbenia....................... 85

CHAPTER 17   Warlock Hahnza.................................. 88

CHAPTER 18   The Black Crystal Ball.......................... 92

CHAPTER 19   The meditation..................................97

CHAPTER 20   The catastrophe................................102

CHAPTER 21   Rebuilding distressed cities...................122

CHAPTER 22   Shameful defeat................................125

CHAPTER 23   The farewell....................................127

CHAPTER 24   Identity confirmation...........................130

CHAPTER 25   The acknowledgment............................135

ILLUSTRATIONS

By Erben Detablan

Figure 1   Prince Petros Domini Hiertocelli................1

Figure 2   "The Prince"...3

Figure 3   Damon Yucca, the evil warrior................ 41

Figure 4   Cain.. 50

Figure 5   Anchor-like stone figurine (Anchret)........54

Figure 6   Prince Kilhazer Pierrum Hiertocelli (the

repugnant twin brother)........................... 66

Figure 7   King Therouso.................................... 79

Figure 8   Queen Harnicella.................................84

Figure 9   An Insurgent in Carbenia.......................87

Figure 10   The Black Crystal Ball...........................91

Figure 11   Richard Blake.....................................96

Figure 12   The Anchret......................................101

Figure 13   Warlock Hahnza.................................121

Figure 14   The Lost Prince of Carbenia..................134

Figure 1: Prince Petros Domini Hiertocelli

INTRODUCTION

It was dark and gloomy outside, an unusual ambiance in the fairy tale-like village full of good-natured and kind-hearted citizens who lived in the Kingdom of Carbenia. Depression and melancholy pervaded the air as the belligerent insurgents marched proudly along the streets, proclaiming their victory and declaring to the people the emergence of a new leadership.

Prince Petros and Warlock Hahnza watched helplessly behind the stained glass window of the secret chamber located inside the palace. This undisclosed cubicle, known only to the king, the queen and Warlock Hahnza, existed exclusively in the advent of contingency. It was a room within a larger room, located in the basement, to the left of the front grand entrance to the palace. This chamber, along with the other stalls situated in the basement, were difficult to track down due to the intricate labyrinth design of the castle's subterranean. Both Prince Petros and Warlock Hahnza had spent the night in the concealed underground compartment to escape the malevolent punishment of the rebels.

All the officials and supporters of the ousted regime had been punished into extinction inside the black crystal ball. They had all been vanished except for the two of them. The kingdom had experienced an excruciating ambush. Only a miracle could save the once majestic and magnificent Kingdom known as Carbenia....

Figure 2:   "The Prince"

CHAPTER 1

It was a breezy, quiet night in the early spring time in Columbus, Ohio as I gazed on the horizon while standing on top of the tallest building in town. I carefully scanned the picturesque view of the city for signs of any criminal activities. I knew that somebody out there would need my help before the night was over.

There it was, two men robbing a convenience store. They had blindfolded and tied the staff working in the store as they ransacked the place. I jumped from the building, ran to the corner next to the store and silently sneaked up behind the robbers as they hurriedly dumped their loot into their getaway car. I punched the first one hard in the jaw when he turned around as he intended to get back into the store. Not expecting the blow from me, he fell on the ground knocked out. The second guy attempted to fight back but I beat him helpless to the ground as well. I then went inside the store and freed the two staff so they could call the police to the scene. I made sure the police got there before I slipped away.

As I was trying to flee the crime scene before anybody

else saw me, I felt this familiar dizziness coming on. I didn't want any publicity of any sort, not yet anyway because I, myself, was quite confused about what was happening to me.

Whoa, there it was again, the dizziness that slowly enveloped my head, making me feel as if everything around me was spinning faster and faster until this persistent and invasive buzzing sound permeated the surrounding..........CRING...........CRING...........CRING...........!

Ahhhh, my alarm clock went off. It was 6:30 AM, time to get up and get ready for work. Okay, what was that? Another weird dream, it just felt so real, as if I were actually there. I could recall every detail that happened in that dream. Everything was so vivid on my mind and I felt so tired waking up. It's like I never went to bed. Whew, this had better come to a stop!

This story was about my life. Some would say that it's interesting and exciting, something that could only take place in a world of pure imagination. I would encourage you to read on and follow the path of my destiny.

My name was Richard Blake, Rick for short. I was a simple guy with a simple, uncomplicated life until somehow everything had gotten so messed up and I had no idea how it got there. I was 31 years old, 6 feet 1 inch tall, 180 lbs, Caucasian, never married, no kids to date and still looking for that one special lady who would make my heart flutter. I thought I was good looking, maybe? Brown hair with deep blue eyes, lean and muscular, well, a little but I didn't flaunt my physique for display. I was actually shy and I tried not to be noticed in public in any way. I was clean cut and wore eye glasses. I didn't smoke and I very seldom drank alcohol. I just did not enjoy the taste and smell of liquor. I was not gay and that was a fact. I was just one of those guys who liked to stay clean, organized and healthy. So how did my life get so complicated? Let's find out...

I worked as an investment consultant for Craig, Sharpe and Thiessel Company for 10 years. I had been an asset to the company since it opened its doors for business about 10 years ago. I enjoyed my work immensely as I tackled tough businessmen strategies on how to grow their investment portfolios. I considered this a challenging but fulfilling career. I designed a plan of action targeting the needs of every clientele coming before our company. I showed my presentation to them, we discussed about the presentation then we agreed on a step by step action plan that they must adhere to in order to help them realize their financial goals. This took time, dedication and discipline to put together. But with proper planning and guidance, most of the time, the end result was very satisfactory to the customers.

At the end of the work day, I went back to my house that had three bedrooms, two full baths, and an attached double car garage. I lived in a decent neighborhood in town. My neighbors consisted mostly of retired folks and other families with maturing children, mostly in their college years or fresh graduates from college. There were no loud noises on the streets, no loud music from cars driving around and very low crime rates reported compared to other neighborhoods. I had been lucky so far and I thanked God everyday for my good fortune.

But then I started having these dreams about me saving the day as I battled criminal activities that were happening in my home state. It had been several months that I kept having these recurrent dreams and they felt so strangely real to me every time. I tried to rationalize that maybe I was just bored silly of my life that I felt the need for speed and danger to complicate my ever so peaceful and predictable existence.

These dreams made me feel untouchable, unbeatable, strong, fearless and indestructible, almost like Superman, yeah! Heck, I even wore a costume and a mask too. My costume was similar to superman's jumpsuit except the colors were black with violet trimmings and violet cape, violet leather boots and violet leather gloves. I also wore a mask that extended to the bridge of my nose as it wrapped around the back of my head, all to hide my identity. And this costume was molded tight on me that it exaggerated my biceps, my six-pack abs, my gluteal muscles and every other muscle there was to brag about.

The costume created an illusion of a perfect piece of a male specimen. I bet even the Incredible Hulk might be threatened by this fantastic show of muscular masterpiece I carried around in that jumpsuit. I was almost positive that body I walked around in was not even mine. This was all but a fiction. I loved it. I was so thrilled in the beginning that I basked in this fantasy. But it had been several months and I was getting physically drained out. I just wanted it to stop, or at least, had a break from it all. If only I could find out how this all started in the first place, then maybe, I could stop them from getting into my sleep every night.

These adventurous escapades started dominating my thoughts even when I was wide awake. I felt confused and baffled. I tried to gain control on how to maintain the life I had always lived without getting caught up in the supernatural dreams and powers I possessed once I closed my eyes into slumber.

CHAPTER 2

I got into the parking lot of the building where I worked. I always wanted to walk around the front door so I could buy a copy of the daily newspaper from the newspaper stand situated several feet away from the main door leading to my office building.

"Good Morning, Mike." I greeted the newspaper stand owner.

"Top of the morning to you," he responded cheerfully. He's an always-jolly, middle-aged, Indian guy, who worked long hours manning his stand all day throughout the week. He kept his humor about him all the time and he had a smile on his face every time I see him.

"How are you today?" He asked genuinely.

"Ah, fine so far I think. How about you?" I replied.

"Oh, just same-o, same-o," he said with that thick Indian accent I have gotten accustomed to all these years.

"Here's your paper, have a good day," he said.

To this I replied, "Thanks, you too."

I proceeded to the main door of the building. I jumped into the elevator taking me to our offices on the 4th floor. Cathy, our receptionist, greeted me pleasantly as I walked in the door.

I went into my office and glanced at my calendar to check my schedule for the day. I would have meetings from 9:30 AM through lunch with some office executives. Then at 2:00 PM, I would meet with a very important client the company had been trying to do business with for years, Mr. James Nelson, from Northern Furnace Company. He was in financial hardship and was trying to gain perspective on how he could possibly turn his company around from going bankrupt. I had been working on some business strategies for his company for two weeks, and I was ready to present my plans to him this day.

It's about 9:00 AM so I had a little time to spare before my day began. I glanced quickly at the newspaper to see what was happening out there that I needed to know about. A brief scan of the front page, I found nothing interesting there. As I turned to the next page, an intriguing article caught my attention. A convenience store on Main Avenue was almost robbed last night. Reading it, the two staff on duty recounted how a masked man with a cape came to their rescue. I carefully scrutinized the tiny picture of the store posted on the paper. It looked very familiar to me, the corner next to the store where I hid in my dream before confronting the thieves, the storefront displays, the entry door to the store, among other small details I could recall about the retail store were visibly all there in that picture. How could this be? It was a dream I had. Could that man with a cape and a mask possibly be me?

My phone rang just then to let me know that our meeting was about ready to start. I gathered my thoughts together and shrugged off the mental image I had about the store incident. I couldn't deal with this thought right now. I had to concentrate on my day's itinerary and dwell on the store incident later at home.

It was difficult concentrating at work today, but I managed somehow to put everything else behind me and went about my day at work as I dealt with issues necessary to put my work first and foremost. I succeeded for now.

It was past 6:00 PM when finally, I was heading home. As I was driving on the road, my thoughts immediately went back to the store incident. Maybe it was all a coincidence. Some guy wearing a cape and a mask came to rescue them. It just coincided with my dream last night. That's it, that should be it, I thought. There was just no explanation how I could be physically present on another location as I was in bed sleeping. Sound reasoning just didn't explain how that could have happened to me or to anybody else. But how did I know some specifics about that incident, the location, the events that led up to it, the staff on duty, the two robbers? Wow, what a coincidence!

I drove up to my driveway and parked in the garage. I went inside my house to the kitchen and started preparing dinner. I turned on the television set to the news watch channel when, again, the news about the aborted robbery on Main Avenue was mentioned. The staff was interviewed and I recalled the frightened faces of those staff when I came in to help them. There's no mistaking I had seen those faces before, if not during last night's scene, then where? These thoughts dominated my entire evening until I got ready for bed at 11:00 PM. Hopefully, there would not be any wild dreams for me tonight.

―   ―   ―   ―   ―   ―   ―   ―   ―

This night, three guys broke into a prominent businessman's home taking hostage the businessman, his wife, daughter and son. Luckily, his daughter, who was 11 years old, was able to call 911 prior to the invaders' coming into her bedroom. Police officers arrived at their home site, surrounded their house and negotiated the release of all four occupants.

The home invaders were ruthless. They shot the businessman as he attempted to protect his family. The wife and the two kids cowered in the corner by the family room as they cried silently and fearfully, watching every move made by the invaders.

I entered a window which was slightly cracked open in the son's bedroom. Silently, I headed downstairs where noises could be heard. I saw all three guys in the main room downstairs. One was watching the three occupants cowering in the corner with a gun pointed at them, the other one was looking out the window inconspicuously, and the third man was on the phone talking to someone. Obviously, he was the leader of the three.

My concern for keeping a low profile was to keep the rest of the family safe and unharmed. I reached out for a decorative vase and threw it in the far corner close to the kitchen to get one of them to move away and check what just happened. The man looking out the window left his post temporarily to find out what it was that broke in the other room. I moved swiftly toward the man watching the family. I punched him hard in the face then landed a few more punches in his diaphragm, knocking him unconscious on the floor.

The other guy came back from the kitchen. He saw me immediately and attempted to shoot me, but I was too fast for him as well. We had a little exchange of punches until he also landed unconscious on the floor.

The third man heard the commotion in the family room. He came quickly and started shooting carelessly everywhere. Fortunately, the three occupants had sense to take cover so no one got hurt. I boldly confronted our attacker, not getting injured by all the bullets he had aimed at me. When close enough, I grabbed and twisted the arm he used to hold the gun until he shouted in pain. I landed a strong slug in his midriff that knocked the air out of him. Then I elbowed him in his back as he slowly descended down onto the floor. I kicked him hard so that he was thrown away a few steps from the family room halfway into the kitchen. I made sure he couldn't fight back anymore at that time.

Finally, I instructed the victims to let the police in so they could take over and make their arrest. The victims came up to me first, crying and hysterical, embraced me and profusely thanked me.

As the police started to enter their home, I made my escape imperceptibly to avoid any publicity.

CHAPTER 3

I woke up the following day at almost 9:30 in the morning. It's Saturday so I slept in a little longer this day. I planned to get some yard work done this morning and some grocery shopping later today.

I turned the TV on as I ate a hearty breakfast. There was a breaking news flash about a home invasion that happened during the night involving a prominent businessman and his family. I was dumbfounded as I listened to the news report. I knew exactly the details of the incident, and I could not believe what I was hearing about.

I wondered what was happening to me. Why did I know all the events of this crime yet again? Was I gaining some kind of a third eye? Or was I really getting transported out of my body while I lay in bed asleep, turning into this other super power guy who was out there at night time helping people in need?

I didn't know what to do, what to say, or who to talk to about all these. Was I going crazy? What should I do? Was it even safe to talk about this to someone else? Like a shrink maybe? No, I had better keep this to myself.

There should be an explanation for all these somehow. But what could it be?

Frustrated and confused, I went about doing my yard work outside as I pondered the events that happened at the home invasion.

Estelle, my next door neighbor, who lived on the left side of my house, was out walking her dog. She saw me and without hesitation, she walked up to me and started making conversation with me. She's retired and she lived by herself with her dog, a German shepherd. Normally, I welcomed her babbling without any problem. But today, I was not in the mood to hear her endless chatter. I was pleasantly relieved when another neighbor, Carl, who was also retired and lived on the right side of my house, came up to us to exchange pleasantries. Luckily, they found a common subject that caught their interest together, and after pleasantly saying goodbye, they proceeded to walk down the street with their dogs in tow.

Next, I saw my other neighbor, Nicholas Hahn, who was about 60 years old and lived right in front of my house. He was getting ready to back out his car from his garage. I waved at him and he returned the favor as he drove away. He moved into the neighborhood about two years ago and had remained very private about his affairs. Even Estelle had not been able to obtain any juicy information about him despite her repeated attempts at engaging him to talk to her. He had always managed to make an excuse to cut short his conversation with any of us.

One time about six months ago, his car broke down as he was about to turn into his driveway. I helped pushed his car into his driveway. As a form of gratitude, he offered me tea while we talked and waited for the car mechanic to arrive.

Inside his home while I was waiting for the tea he was preparing for me, I noticed this black crystal ball about the size of a small basketball, maybe about eight inches in circumference, sitting on a vase for support, carefully displayed on his curio cabinet. It was captivating although it didn't have any other decoration or color mixed in that would give a little life to it. It was just plain dark black in color but was solid rock on the outside.

I moved closer to inspect it when somehow, I thought, I saw a glimmer of light starting to show on the inside. Then it seemed as though a veil was removed, revealing what looked like a village to me, full of suffering people as they looked back at me. It was strange that I saw all these people tucked in inside that little ball. The look on their faces, that sad, pitiful expression I gathered from looking through the ball, was heart breaking.

I was so mesmerized in this moment that I didn't realize Nicholas was standing next to me. He was watching me with a surprised expression on his face, almost like he wanted to cry. His face flushed with anticipation and apprehension at the same time. His hand shook when he handed me the tea cup.

"Are you okay, Nicholas?" I asked.

17

"Oh yeah, I'm fine," he said nervously, still staring at me, like he was searching for something on my face. It appeared to me that he was profoundly affected by what he had witnessed. I, on the other hand, was intrigued. Was that real, what I thought I saw inside the ball?

"That's a cool ball you have there. Where did you get it from?" I asked him casually.

"I got it from a very far place about 30 years ago. I'm actually keeping it until the rightful owner comes along to claim it," he replied meaningfully as he continued to stare at me with that probing, hopeful look in his eyes.

"It's an interesting piece of decoration," I said.

"Well, it's more than that. It's a very valuable piece that holds life and sustains that life from extinction," he responded mysteriously.

His response triggered a lot of questions in me, but common courtesy told me not to probe any further. I did not want to make him feel uncomfortable, especially as we were just getting acquainted. Of course, he could always tell me more about it if he so wished. But he did not pursue this topic as well. Instead, he asked about my childhood and my parents. I thought perhaps he just wanted to keep the conversation going, so I obliged.

"I was born and raised in Toledo, Ohio. My parents were both teachers, so I learned to keep my studies a priority early in life." I started telling him. "We lived in a small house by the lake. It was peaceful and quiet, with trees and shrubs surrounding our property. My parents loved the solitude and tranquility that place afforded us. I, too, enjoyed that setting. I always looked forward to visiting them when I had time."

"I moved here to Columbus to pursue college at Ohio State University. I started working for the company I still work for to this day right after graduation. I liked it here, so I have been living here for over 14 years now," I continued.

"How are your parents, if I may ask? " He inquired.

"They are deceased. They had an unfortunate car accident about two years ago. They died on the spot." I answered.

"I'm sorry to hear that," he said.

"Do you have any siblings?" He queried.

"No, I'm an only child. So were both of my parents. My father's mother, Grandma Josie, is staying at a nursing home back in Toledo. She has Alzheimer's disease, so she does not even recognize me anymore. I try to visit her about every three months or so."

I didn't know why I was telling this man my life story. Even more intriguing was that he actually seemed really interested in knowing more about me. I wondered why. He asked what my childhood was like, how my parents treated me, and if I had a good life growing up.

"My parents were wonderful to me. They were kind,

loving and generous to me, even when at times, we were financially strapped. They attempted to provide for all my needs. They were hardworking people." I started saying.

"I had a decent life growing up. I had a few friends I hung out with back then. I still manage to talk to them sometimes to this day," I finished saying.

Just then the car mechanic walked in, so I got ready to leave. Before I left his place though, I glanced at the black crystal ball once more. There was something about that decoration that caught my interest. I would definitely ask him more about that ball in time, I told myself.

CHAPTER 4

The crime-fighting dreams continued on night after night. From kidnapping, robbery, vandalism, killing incidents, drug bust, on and on, the dreams kept coming in every night.

I noticed a new development though. I had this feeling someone was watching me from afar in my dreams. I couldn't quite confirm this discovery just yet, but I had this strong awareness of someone else's presence other than mine and the people involved in the crime scene. I felt like I was being observed, how I planned my attacks, how I carried out my plans and the end results of my plans were being evaluated. My thinking process and my ability to get the work done were being analyzed and considered carefully. But why did that matter to anyone else as long as crimes were getting solved, bad guys were put to jail and good guys were protected? Why was there a need to analyze my intellectual capabilities? Who could be watching me, taking such interest in me to invade my dreams on a regular basis as well? Why me?

Tonight as I watched the city on top of a building, I noticed a man and a woman arguing loudly in the parking lot of a nearby restaurant. Then there was a struggle as if the man were forcing the woman to get into his car. The woman then yelled for help, so I came on down and showed myself to them. I asked if everything was okay. The man yelled back at me to stay away and to mind my own business. The woman had tears falling down her cheeks. She was obviously upset.

"Ma'am, are you all right?" I asked her.

The man interrupted again, "I said, mind your own business. Go! Scram! Leave us alone if you know what's good for you, hear me!?"

He shouted loudly, threatening me. Obviously, this man had too much to drink. As if to emphasize his anger, he started walking toward me, swaying slightly as he walked closer to confront me.

I stood firmly where I was, crossed my arms across my chest, and amusedly watched him as he came closer to me. His hands were formed into fists, poised to throw punches at me, face stern, eyes smoldering and lips pursed, all of these meant to intimidate a person, of course, but not me.

An arm's length away from me, he attempted to cast his first strike at me. To this I merely extended my left arm past across his back and pushed him to the ground. He stumbled unsteadily to the ground, got back up clumsily on to his feet, and with all his might, started throwing flying kicks in the air. Alternating with this awkward performance, he moved his arms back and forth in front of him, both hands still formed tightly into fists as he aspired to give me the beatings he had in mind to inflict on me. I extended my right arm across his forehead and without an effort, kept his intended punches away from me into the air while he persisted on.

This ridiculous show of kickboxing lasted for several minutes. Finally, I had enough of this ludicrous exhibition, so I hit him hard in his belly, enough to get him gasping for air while he knelt down on the ground.

"Do you want more?" I asked him casually, pretending to be so bored with him and his tactics.

"No," he said, turning his head from side to side, admitting his humiliating loss.

"I hope you learned your lesson tonight. Do not force anybody to do anything against his or her will. Drunk or sober, you are responsible for your own actions. And by the way, have some respect for yourself too. Man, you're wasted!" I told him disgustedly.

The man gave me a dirty look, giving off the impression "if looks could kill………," but that's all he did. He just sat carelessly in the parking lot. His face remained disgruntled and infuriated but he kept his silence.

I took a deep breath, shrugged my shoulders and walked away from him. I turned my attention to the woman in the parking lot as she cried quietly sitting by her car. She looked up as I came closer, stood up and thanked me generously for coming to her rescue.

I could clearly see her face this time. She had an adorable, pretty face that kept me captivated for a while. Her eyes were small but expressive, nose tiny but straight and formed high, lips full and slightly pouting, cheeks flushed maybe from the events of the night and hair flowing freely on her shoulders. She mumbled some words to me, but I was lost in my thoughts about her that I did not comprehend what she just said. I watched her get into her car then she drove away. I realized then that I did not even know her name and how I wished I asked her name so I could maybe look her up online sometime. I really wanted to see her again.

"Ahhh," I let out a sigh of regret. My eyes followed her moving car as it disappeared down the road.

CHAPTER 5

At work the following day, I kept thinking about the lady I met in my dreams. I wondered if I would ever see her again. I had not felt this interest in meeting someone special for so long that I actually felt a sense of loss for not knowing if she really existed or if she was just a figment of my imagination. I felt a tinge of sadness just thinking about what could have been if we met in person in this real world instead of meeting her in my dream.

"Hey Rick, we're going out to Barry's tonight. Do you want to come along?" Pete, a co-worker, asked me. Barry's was a bar in town that was known for having good food and for being a great place to meet people.

"No, I think I'll take a rain check tonight. I'm beat." I declined purposely. I was not into the bar scene, especially because I did not enjoy drinking liquor. Pete had invited me countless times in the past about going to bars to meet people. He's also into dating sites on the internet, hoping to meet someone he would finally settle down with.

Between work and my full time crime fighting fantasies, I actually didn't have any energy left in me to do anything else. I felt like I was awake 24/7 the past 7 or 8 months now.

I still didn't see this coming to an end anytime soon. I hadn't really figured out what was causing me to have these dreams every night.

I went to the break room to get some coffee after lunch. Two of our office secretaries, Cathy and Mary, were excited about some news they were reading in the paper. I overheard them saying something about a masked man with a cape who helped people in distress at night time.

"Oh Mary, look here…" Cathy said to Mary as she pointed to something in the paper.

"Oh…he's gorgeous! Look at his biceps, and that six-pack abs! Whew! My, my, my, look at his butt, man……!" Mary replied breathlessly.

They both giggled like teenagers and these women were in their fifties to say the least. I found myself looking over their shoulders to the photos they were lusting over out of curiosity. And there they were, to my surprise, I was looking at my photos wearing my tight jumpsuit in black, my unmentionables visibly enhanced to these leering witches' delight!

My goodness, I had been exposed! Well, my superhero counterpart had been compromised. I had been very careful about not being seen in public in my dreams. How could anybody have taken those photos of me without me knowing about it? And how could this be happening?

Again, why was I in those photos? I fought crimes in my dreams. Why were there photos of me in costume printed clearly in the newspaper with reports of the incidents I helped prevent from happening in my dreams? This was so confusing! I was starting to get terrified by these revelations. My dreams were actually happening in real life!

As I walked away from the break room, I felt the need to cover myself up because I didn't want people to recognize me in those photos. Granted, my true identity hopefully was still kept a secret by wearing a mask. I had been truly shaken up by those photos. The reality was that there was no denying this time that the masked man with a cape was really me.

I hurriedly left the office once it was time to go. I did not want anyone to notice how nervously I had been behaving the entire afternoon. I avoided any kind of interaction with anybody whether in the office or outside the parking lot, or even in my neighborhood as I drove safely back into my house. I wanted to read more about the reports and look closely at those photos in the privacy of my home.

As I was reading through the collective reports about the masked man with a cape on the internet, I realized people had been talking about this unknown hero for some time now. The photos though, had just started to come to the surface. A certain reporter, John Hemmings, just recently got lucky to have witnessed a crime scene that started as he was walking past midnight in the downtown area on his way back to his apartment. He saw two guys vandalizing vacant houses then setting them on fire. He called the police as they were working on the third house.

Suddenly, he saw me fist fighting with the two bad guys as I prevented them from doing more harm to the properties. He did not realize it was the unknown hero at first, he just thought some man braved the vandals' attacks. He started taking pictures of the incident for his news report. Once the actual prints came out, then he realized he got pictures of the anonymous masked man.

"Oh, how fortunate I am," he proudly thought to himself, "The elusive, unknown hero! Finally, some photos to prove his existence. This is an exclusive report indeed!"

The photos did not really reveal too much of me. Yes, it proved there was a man in costume with a mask fighting bad guys. There were no up close photos of the "unknown hero" to even slightly give anyone a clue about his true identity. It showed his physique undoubtedly, enough to engage the curiosity of even the most conservative girl in town. But otherwise, my identity was safe, for now anyway. Next time, I might not be so lucky. How could I be more careful to avoid having my pictures taken in the future? I realized that I couldn't control people from taking photos of things that captured their interest. So it was up to me to be extra cautious about maintaining my anonymity.

CHAPTER 6

My crime fighting dreams had crossed borders to include neighboring states of Ohio. I was in Charlotte, North Carolina one night to prevent two trains from colliding with each other caused by faulty railroad tracks. On another night, I was in Virginia preventing a private plane from crashing down due to bad weather. Then one night I was in New York saving a fishing boat from capsizing. More and more states were witnessing my amazing acts of valor.

Meanwhile in California, several news reports had emerged about another man in costume with a mask who had been wreaking havoc on some occasions, causing major problems and heartaches to multitudes of people and business establishments. Theaters were set on fire, a stadium collapsed when support pillars were purposely damaged, drinking water was contaminated with Escherichia Coli bacteria, poisonous snakes were dumped by the dozens in a children's playground, the list of malicious disturbances went on.

These incidents were just recently thought to be interconnected, caused by the same man after thorough investigations were conducted. A distinct mark that looked like a triple inverted 6 was always left behind on every incident he was involved in.

A public announcement was made for people to be more vigilant of their surroundings and to contact the police department immediately for any signs of suspicious activities.

Back in Ohio, I fell asleep early tonight because of sheer exhaustion from not getting enough rest at night time. In my sleep, I dreamed I was standing inconspicuously outside a restaurant while I observed a couple of people having dinner inside the restaurant by the window.

Then I realized I was watching the same girl I met weeks ago at a parking lot of another restaurant in town. I was excited to see her again and was looking forward to finding out more information about her this time. I listened intently to their conversation using my extra-sensorial hearing power. I found out that the woman and her date met through an online dating site called Singles Match and this was the first time they met in person.

Her name was Angeline Laurel. She's an Asian-American lady, born and raised in Hawaii who migrated to Ohio with her family in the year 2000. The move was necessitated when her father was promoted as a general manager of an electrical power plant. Angeline was a statistician by profession and she worked for a pharmaceutical company in town.

"Hmmm, smart girl. I like that." I whispered to myself as I

continued to watch them. I could sense that I was getting interested in her more than ever. I had no choice but to admire her from a distance, for the time being anyway.

Their date progressed slowly. Their conversation flowed mostly on friendly "get-to-know-you-more" topics as they dined and wined through the night.

"I'm just gonna go to the ladies' room." Angeline said to her date.

"Sure, I'll be here when you get back." Tom, her date, replied politely.

In her absence from their table, I noticed that Tom slipped something into Angeline's drink. He carefully looked around to make sure nobody had seen his move. This observation made me pay closer attention to the incident that was about to unfold.

I even thought about barging in on Tom to confront him about what he just did. But Angeline came back from the ladies' room before I could carry out my plan. Besides, I really did not want to create a scene where a lot of people could witness my appearance.

The couple continued on their date until half past 10 PM. Angeline was very drowsy, leaning heavily on Tom as they got ready to leave the restaurant. Tom held Angeline close to his side, his right arm wrapped around her waist possessively as he guided her to the parking lot into his car. She was fast asleep in his car as he drove away from the restaurant. He started heading back to her place. I followed them closely, flying up in the air, maintaining close visual contact the entire time.

Thirty minutes later, Tom came to a halt in front of Angeline's house. Angeline remained asleep in the car so Tom carried her into her home, laid her down on the sofa and sat beside her. He started caressing her hair, her face and her lips. He leaned forward to kiss her when he felt a strong hand grabbed him by his collar. He turned around to see a man wearing a jumpsuit with a cape and a mask.

He read about this "unknown hero" in the papers, but he really did not expect to see him at this inopportune time.

"Dude, let go of me!" He said, exasperated that his plan was rudely interrupted by this stranger.

"You can go now," I spoke quietly, but I was seething with controlled anger directed at him.

Tom knew he was no match with this man physically. So he scrammed out of Angeline's home in a hurry. But before he left I threatened, "Don't you ever come anywhere near her again, hear me?"

Tom looked at me sharply, extremely irritated but in no way going to even attempt to say anything back to me. He knew it would be better to leave unscathed than to start a losing battle.

After the bamboozler left, I looked over to where Angeline was. She remained peacefully asleep, oblivious to the interrupted assault that had almost befallen her. I checked her place for any signs of suspicious activity. Then when I was satisfied that she was safe inside her home, I decided that it was time to leave. I locked the doors behind me before I left her place.

As I walked pass the front window of her flat, I glanced at her one more time. I felt my heart skip a beat, coupled with this intense yearning to get to know her more. I would definitely look her up again in the coming days. This time, I will introduce myself to her as Rick, the ordinary guy, the guy who had been captivated by her unassuming beauty and grace.

"Hopefully, her record of dating scumbags will finally come to an end." I wished earnestly.

CHAPTER 7

This Saturday, I woke up with no desire to do anything outside my home. I did house chores in the morning, had a leisurely lunch, and then browsed on the internet at the Singles Match website in the afternoon. I purposely searched for Angeline Laurel on the list of available singles.

There she was, photo and some detailed information about her, with matching invitation from the website's developer to start communicating with her for a nominal fee. Normally, this way of meeting people did not spark an interest in me, but because of Angeline, I was more than willing to pay the membership fee just to have a chance at getting to know her more.

"You've got mail!" my computer informed me.

I immediately opened my email, hoping to hear back from Angeline after I sent her an email about two hours ago through the dating site.

"Hey, how's it going? Thanks for sending me a note. I read your profile here on Singles Match and I think it would be great to talk sometime. Here's my cell number,

(614) 785-4403, give me a buzz sometime. Thanks. Angeline"

I was so excited to hear from her. Finally, I would have a chance to actually meet her as me, Rick. I would call her tonight, I thought to myself.

"Hello?" Angeline greeted hesitantly on the phone.

"Angeline?" I asked softly.

"This is she," she replied carefully.

"Hey, it's Rick, Rick Blake from Singles Match…" I informed her.

"Hi, Rick. How are you?" She then said sweetly.

"I'm good, thanks. And you?" I replied pleasantly. I tried to control my enthusiasm so as not to appear too needy and desperate at the same time. Also, I didn't want to scare her off in any way.

"Fine, thanks," was her reply.

We talked for over an hour like old friends, sharing funny jokes and experiences, comparing notes on likes and dislikes related to food, friends, work and just about anything to keep the conversation flowing. She seemed funny and easy to talk to, yet intelligent and knowledgeable when more serious topics were discussed. We enjoyed chatting on the phone so we decided to talk again sometime next week, then possibly meet for lunch on Saturday.

Time came quickly to meet with Angeline for lunch at Don Juan's restaurant. I came in about 20 minutes early to get a table that would provide the most privacy and comfort conducive to a relaxing and enjoyable meeting, as we indulge in great food and great company.

She came in wearing a pink sundress, looking as cute as a button. I waved at her to get her attention. She waved back at me after she recognized me from the photos I had posted on the dating site. As I watched her walk toward me, I realized my heart was racing fast in my chest and I felt short of breath as she came closer to where I was.

"Rick?" She asked.

"Yes it's me, Angeline." I replied as I helped her to her chair.

"You look good," I said as I handed her a bouquet of pink tulips.

"Thank you," she said shyly.

At lunch, our conversation flowed effortlessly. But at times, I could not help but stare at her. I had to admit I was attracted to her from the first time I saw her in the parking lot. And she was even lovelier in the day time, especially in this moment that she was not in distress like our initial encounter. Her face was glowing like the sun, eyes clear and expressive, lips curled to a smile revealing a perfect set of pearly, white teeth and hair soft and smooth on her shoulders.

I felt a sudden urge to lean over and kiss her, but I held off. I told myself that it was certainly not the right time for this kind of behavior. I did not want to come on too strong and give her the wrong impression about me. I did not want to ruin a very promising relationship that might develop between us.

Our lunch date lasted for almost three hours. It was amazing how much I enjoyed meeting her for the first time. I hated to end our date, but we both had other things to do to keep our busy lives in order. We did arrange to meet another day so we could get to know each other more.

CHAPTER 8

Angeline and I had been seeing each other for about three months. We had gone to a lot of different events and attractions like wine tasting, visiting amusement parks, museums, attending concerts and plays, watching movies together and other fun-filled activities. Being with her made me feel so alive and happy. It's like my life was suddenly filled with a new found excitement and meaning, something I had not felt for so long after living alone since my parents passed away. It's like living in a dream and I didn't want to wake up from this fantasy.

One lovely, quiet evening after having dinner with Angeline, we strolled through the park hand in hand, silently enjoying the serene, scenic view of the lake. Suddenly, out of nowhere, five masked men sneaked up on us, knives on hand, surrounding us, moving in closer and closer to where we were. At arm's length, one of them grabbed Angeline away from me, then the others attacked me all at the same time. Angeline struggled to fight her attacker but she was stabbed in her side, sending her slowly descending to the ground. I, on the other hand, started fighting back to my surprise. As far as I know, I didn't know martial arts or any kind of self-defense. Yet, I was fighting like a pro! I was throwing punches all over the attackers and I gave them a roundhouse kick, knocking down four of them all at once. Then I ran over toward Angeline and her attacker, pulled the arm he used to stab Angeline with and twisted it hard until he shrieked in agonizing pain.

Once all five attackers were down to the ground, I turned my attention to Angeline who was bleeding profusely. I called 911 for medical emergency assistance, as well as to report the incident of the attack.

At the hospital, Angeline was rushed to the operating room for a much needed surgery to control her bleeding and repair the wound she sustained from getting stabbed. I waited outside the operating room in the waiting area until she was transferred to the recovery room, then finally to the intensive care unit for close monitoring. She was hooked up to a life support and other tubes to keep her alive. My heart was aching so badly seeing her so helpless and vulnerable. I was so angry at myself for not being able to protect her from this tragedy. If she did not make it through this ordeal, I didn't know how I could forgive myself. God, please help her.....

‒   ‒   ‒   ‒   ‒   ‒   ‒   ‒

It had been several days after the incident and I had been coming in every night to visit Angeline at the hospital. She remained unresponsive and had continued to be on life support. I missed her so much, the way she talked and laughed, the way she used to make me smile with just about anything, the way she looked at me, the smell of her hair, the taste of her lips, how I longed for those times when we were together, doing all kinds of fun things or just hanging out at my place or hers, chatting about anything under the sun. Please God, help her recover from this, I prayed ardently. Please send her back to me.

—   —   —   —   —   —   —

Thinking back on the night of the assault, I was still perplexed as to how I defeated all five assailants. How did I learn to fight like that? And why did I feel so strong and mighty when I confronted them, almost like I felt confident that they were no match to my strength and power? I did not have any training in martial arts at all. Maybe it was that surge of energy I read about that people experienced when they were confronted with impossible situations such as carrying a refrigerator in case of fire, swimming for miles to get to safety when in danger of drowning and other circumstances like that. That's got to be the answer to this remarkable performance in martial arts. And it was a much needed help at a time such as that.

Figure 3:   Damon Yucca - The Evil Warrior

CHAPTER 9

In California, Damon Yucca, a formidable, ruthless, heartless criminal defense attorney, was getting ready for a high profile case involving his client, a corrupt politician, who had been accused of murdering his business partner. Currently, the accused politician, Jerome Briggs, was incarcerated at a maximum security state prison facility in Pelican Bay, California. This was a tough case since all evidence on hand had incriminated the politician. But Damon was not perturbed. He had defended many accused clients in the past and his record of winning cases had not been stained.

Damon believed in the philosophy that a person was innocent until proven guilty. He managed to turn evidence around to favor his clients regardless of whether his clients were truly at fault or not. More often than not, he set criminals free. This was the thrill he longed for; he liked to challenge the truth. The more twisted the truth was presented, the greater satisfaction he would get from it.

This day, Damon was getting ready to go to court for a

hearing. He would meet his client in court. He had all the evidence he needed to win this case once and for all. He was confident today would be the day his client would be set free.

In court, Damon informed his client about the details of his presentation to the jury and the judge presiding over the case. His client listened intently, impressed beyond words about how his attorney managed to concoct a scenario so believable, so convincing and so full of lies that only the people involved in the crime would be able to tell the difference. Of course, he would go along with this plan of action. After all, his future was at stake here. He was actually fighting for his life. If proven guilty, he could face capital punishment, the death penalty.

Damon stood up, eyes fixed on the judge as he said, "Your honor, I would like to call my primary witness to the stand."

Damon turned around as he introduced his witness, his client's mistress, Miss Jeanette Collins. Everybody who was familiar with the case gasped with disgust as they watched Jeanette Collins emerge from behind the double doors and walk toward the stand. The client's wife, who was in the crowd giving support to her accused husband, trembled as she controlled her anger concerning the unfolding of this illicit affair for the first time. Tears welled up in her eyes, blinding her sight temporarily.

Jeanette raised her right arm to take oath to tell the truth and nothing but the truth before sitting down to take the stand.

"Miss Collins, would you tell the court about where Mr. Briggs was on the night of the murder?" Damon asked Jeanette.

"Jerome Briggs was with me in my apartment on the night of the murder. He came in at around 7:00 PM and stayed overnight until he left early in the morning at around 6:00 AM." Jeanette stated as a matter of fact.

"Can you prove your statement?" Damon interrogated.

"Yes, that night was special to us since we were celebrating our first year anniversary. We recorded our love making on a video tape." Jeanette confirmed, as she handed a copy of the video to Damon.

Damon handed the video tape to the judge who gave it to the court clerk for proper handling and viewing.

While watching the erotic, passionate and revealing video, Jerome's wife, Suzanne, stood up and left the court room. That was too much to take in. This would be the last time she would ever be fooled by her husband again, she thought to herself. "I was so stupid to trust him again." She whispered silently to herself as she drove away from the court house.

Damon pointed out to the court the time period the tape was recorded which happened to coincide with the time the murder was committed on the other side of town, about 30 minutes away. Although not admissible in court as proof but has legal "value", Damon presented a copy of the apartment's CCTV which showed Jerome going in to the apartment at 7:18 PM and leaving at 6:10 AM the following day, proving Jeanette's earlier statement.

Damon also informed the court that the CCTV on hand had inclusive coverage of the eleven hour time frame involved that started when the defendant entered Jeanette Collins' apartment building until the time he left the following day. The CCTV was available for supervised viewing by the jurors and the judge assigned to the case for further evaluation and study.

Damon emphasized that his client, Jerome Briggs, stayed with Jeanette Collins all night long and the CCTV would provide footage pertinent to this statement.

"My next door neighbor, Michael Harmon, spoke to Jerome while waiting for the elevator to come up that morning. They went out of the building together." Jeanette informed the court.

Damon told the court that Michael Harmon was in attendance as well to confirm his brief encounter with the accused.

After Damon was satisfied with Jeanette's testimony, the attorney of the bereaved family, Harold Smith, was given a chance to cross-examine the witness.

Harold Smith was surprised by the appearance of this major witness. He was not expecting this sudden turn of events. All evidence pointed to Jerome being guilty until now. He attempted to collect his thoughts together as he conducted his cross-examination of Jeanette Collins. But there was no loophole to present to the court that Jeanette was not telling the truth. Her statement and evidence were so strong and affirmative to prove that Jerome was not guilty as presumed on earlier court hearings. With this current testimony, Jerome Briggs would undoubtedly be a free man at the end of this session. And sure enough, he was acquitted from the case.

That night, Damon and Jerome celebrated their victory in the privacy of Jerome's mansion. They invited high class prostitutes to entertain them and the place was overflowing with illegal drugs and alcohol.

They were passed out until mid-morning the following day. Upon waking up, Damon went back to his place.

—   —   —   —   —   —   —

Damon Yucca was a ruggedly handsome, German-American man in his mid thirties, about 6 feet 6 inches tall, very muscular in appearance and extremely domineering in every way. He was also a very smart man but unfortunately, he used his intelligence to promote evil and malicious acts.

Damon had a hard life growing up. He was raised without knowing who his parents were. He was left on the side of the road beside the mailbox of a temporary shelter for boys when he was just a newborn. The shelter was his home until he ran away when he was 13 years of age. He'd had enough of the abuse and neglect from the shelter, so he turned to the streets and became homeless for a while. He started working everywhere doing menial jobs so he could have money to buy food to eat. But those jobs were few and temporary, so he did not have money a lot of times. He would scavenge for food scraps in some unlikely places to satisfy his hunger. He was always in need of even the most basic things in life such as food, shelter and clothing. He had nothing to eat and drink most of the time. And people would look at him with distaste because he smelled and was very dirty. They turned away from him every time they saw him.

Damon was constantly fighting for survival ever since he could remember. This made him want to become successful in life someday.

When he turned 16 years old, he joined a gang that was in the business of selling and supplying illegal drugs nationwide. He was committed and diligent to his work, so he climbed up the ladder, becoming one of the drug lords in the country.

But Damon had great ambitions and aspirations so he went back to school and studied all the way. He graduated   from Harvard Law School with high honors.

He continued to work hard day and night. Finally, he attained his ultimate goal, to be a top-notch, undefeated, undisputed criminal defense attorney in the nation.

Because of his background, Damon learned to be tough and heartless when dealing with people. His work was the only thing that mattered to him. It was the only thing that had kept him company all these years, and it had given him all the advantages in life he now enjoyed.

Damon had maintained a good relationship with the gangsters he used to work for. He frequently referred new clients to them, and he represented them in court whenever there was a need for him to do so.

Damon had ventured into other things as well. He had founded a website called mindinterconnect.com where criminals, ex convicts and other sociopaths were encouraged to join. The website contained all kinds of vulgarities and obscenities whether in words, photos, videos or other expressions of indecency. The number of members who were joining had multiplied by the hundreds on a daily basis. Some members were just spectators, curious to see what it was all about; some were entertained by the jokes and statements posted on the website; some enjoyed the games that were presented; and others were active participants in instigating offensive display of behavior and morality. The members were not aware that there was a program installed on the website that slowly brainwashed the members to commit evil deeds.

Lastly, Damon had a deep dark secret that he kept to himself. When he fell asleep, he would transform into this evil warrior who was very strong and powerful, carrying what looked like an anchor for boats attached to a long, heavy chain. This device was called *Anchret* and he used this as a tool for destroying anything when he was in action, spreading vicious wrongdoings.

Damon started having dreams about causing major trouble and destruction to people and business establishments, right at the time he created his website, mindinterconnect.com. He met a man in his dream on the night he transformed into an evil warrior for the first time. The man he met in his dream was the first one to commit a murder in the history of mankind. This man was no other than Cain, the first born son of Adam and Eve.

Figure 4: Cain

CHAPTER 10

According to the Bible in Genesis 4, Adam and Eve's first born son was named Cain. Cain had a brother named Abel. God was pleased with Abel and his offerings but not Cain's. So Cain became very angry with Abel and killed him. God punished Cain to become "a restless wanderer on the earth."

Cain said to the Lord, "My punishment is more than I can bear. Today you are driving me from the land, and I will be hidden from your presence; I will be a restless wanderer on the earth, and whoever finds me will kill me."

But the Lord said to him, "Not so, anyone who kills Cain will suffer vengeance seven times over." Then the Lord put a mark on Cain so that no one who found him would kill him. So Cain went out from the Lord's presence and lived in the land of Nod, east of Eden...

Indignant and vindictive, Cain sought the devil and made a deal with him about proliferating and perpetuating wickedness on earth. He promised the devil that he would create a new world where Cain would be worshipped as god on earth while the devil would be known as the omnipotent, supreme master of the universe.

The devil agreed to this proposal, so he accorded Cain with phenomenal powers to help him accomplish this goal. With the devil by his side, Cain had gained confidence, strength and determination to turn this proposition into reality.

Cain had survived for generations after generations on earth, spreading evil on mankind. His presence could be traced back to all major catastrophes in human history. He played an important part as a secret adviser to Adolf Hitler, Joseph Stalin, Saddam Hussein, Osama Bin Laden, Fidel Castro, to mention a few.

Cain had maintained his presence in the background all these years, keeping a low profile as to keep his identity confidential. This was the reason why he used corrupt men of power to promulgate and scatter wickedness on earth. Cain was made stronger every time men commit sinful acts. Their weakness was his strength. Their downfall would lift him up to glory.

Cain saw great potential in Damon when he created a social network online encouraging sociopaths to join. He was impressed with Damon's audacity and tenacity related to his life's choices and actions. His character and careless disregard for morality and righteousness had led him to believe that Damon would fit perfectly as his partner in crime.

Cain appeared in Damon's dream to engage Damon to take part in his conquest for a new world. Cain had placed an anchor-like stone figurine that had black, red and orange colors on Damon's display cabinet. Cain kept a close watch on this precious item to make sure that it remained safe at all times. Unknown to Damon, this was his source of power as well as his destruction in the event this figurine was destroyed.

Figure 5: Anchor-like stone figurine (Anchret)

CHAPTER 11

Meanwhile in Ohio, Angeline was recovering progressively. She was off the ventilator, had been transferred to a regular nursing floor and was awake and verbally responsive. Rick had remained faithful in visiting her every evening after work.

This evening, while waiting for Angeline to wake up, Rick fell asleep on the couch inside her room. He dreamed he was in California witnessing a stampede caused by the collapse of the Hollywood sign located on Mount Lee in the Hollywood Hills area of the Santa Monica Mountains. The sign overlooked the Hollywood district of Los Angeles.

People were running in different directions to keep safe. Rick noted that each letter comprising the sign was individually being uprooted and thrown in the air. He observed closely how this was happening. To his surprise, he saw this enormous figure at the base of every letter smashing each letter with something that looked like a boat anchor made of heavy metal attached to a long, large chain.

Rick swiftly moved to confront the perpetrator and just

then, the enormous figure noticed him. They stared at each other for a few seconds, sizing up each other, paying close attention to how each one would measure up in the impending fight.

Damon turned to face Rick boldly. His full attention was given to this intruder, his wrath apparent behind his stony look. He raised his arm holding the *Anchret* above his head, spinning it slowly at first, then gradually getting faster until it was in full speed, strong and forceful, suspended in the air. He started running towards Rick, eyes burning with rage, ready to crush his opponent.

Rick stood his ground, arms on his waist, waiting for his attacker to come closer, not a hint of apprehension in him, determined to win this battle. When Damon was close enough that his *Anchret* could have hit Rick, Rick flew up in the air, landing behind Damon's back. He pushed Damon hard in the back, causing him to stumble a little on his feet. Damon however, easily regained his composure. He turned around to face Rick once again. Damon started spinning his *Anchret* once more, this time spinning it at a 45 degree angle just above his forehead. He hit Rick on his side, sending him rolling down to the ground. Damon continued to chase Rick, the *Anchret* still spinning as it got closer to Rick once again.

Rick, who was sitting on the ground as he steadied himself, reached out his arm and grabbed the chain close to the head of the *Anchret* as hard as he could muster. He pulled it toward himself with all his might; then, when Damon was within reach, he stretched out his right leg and kicked Damon forcefully, sending him sliding down to the ground, his bottom dragging across the grassy slope of the hill.

Rick stood up, holding the *Anchret* tight as he started to whirl the device above his head, intending to take his revenge on Damon with it. He then noticed a couple of helicopters circling around them with reporters onboard. They were recording this encounter as they reported the live news on television. Also briefly, he turned his head to look directly at the shadow he thought had been watching him all along. To his astonishment, he saw his neighbor's face, Nicholas Hahn, sternly observing them as well.

This discovery distracted Rick's concentration. Nonetheless, he continued advancing toward Damon, intending to finally end this combat. Just when he was about to give his final blow, he heard a sound coming from somewhere, faint at first then becoming clearer and louder, calling out his name, Rick….Rick….Rick….!

Rick woke up to hear Angeline calling him. He realized he was still in the hospital waiting for Angeline to wake up when he dozed off. And now Angeline was wide awake, was excited to see him and to speak with him. Rick was happy to oblige but was secretly wishing he could have finished off his enemy in his dream. Now, he would never know what became of that unknown adversary.

CHAPTER 12

The night when Rick came home after visiting Angeline at the hospital, he had some thoughts he'd wanted to ponder.

"Who was that unknown madman, purposely creating trouble to inflict pain and suffering on people? Why was he doing that? And what happened to him after I disappeared from the scene? Did he continue demolishing the Hollywood sign? How about the people, did they get injured? Were there many destroyed properties caused by the demolition? Also, why was Nicholas Hahn in my dream? Was he the mysterious shadow I have seen watching me in my dreams? What business was it of his to observe my crime fighting engagements, and how was he able to penetrate my dreams?" All these unanswered questions bothered him seriously.

"I hope I could go back to that same dream tonight when I fall asleep." Rick thought to himself.

Unable to sleep just yet, Rick turned the television set on. There in the news, he saw the video of the incident that happened on Mount Lee involving the Hollywood sign.

It showed what remained of the sign, the destruction of the properties caused by the flying letters that came from the signage, interviews of people who witnessed the commotion and some footage of the showdown between the madman and himself. There were no close-up photos of them, so it was hard to tell who they really were. Also, both of them wore masks to protect their identities.

"But who was that man?" This thought persisted on Rick's mind. It was a strange sight to see another character that seemed to come from a different world altogether.

"Could it be possible that he was from another planet? If so, could there be any more like him here on earth?" Rick ruminated over this possibility.

After Rick had disappeared from the scene, his opponent seemed to disappear as well. The reporters stated that somehow the two characters fighting on the scene just vanished into thin air. No trace of them could be found anywhere, and people were perplexed at this mystery.

–   –   –   –   –   –   –

When Rick finally fell asleep, his dream took him to a different scenario. There was a multiple vehicular accident on Highway 755 caused by a 16 wheeler truck that lost control due to brake malfunction. The truck had slammed innumerable vehicles on the road until finally it skidded off the road into the ditch that led to wooded trees further up.

Several people died on the spot. Some people were hurt badly and were trapped inside their vehicles. Some were slightly injured but were in shock, while others got out unscathed and started helping other victims the best way they could manage.

Rick started helping out, freeing trapped victims from their vehicles to safer grounds, directing others who were capable of helping how they could assist injured victims, and lifting other victims from the crash site to safety. All these life-saving measures he carried on until police officers and paramedics finally came to the rescue. Then he discreetly made his escape.

Before Rick left the accident site, he spotted Nicholas Hahn again in the background. This time, he was not hiding behind the scenes anymore. He boldly showed himself to Rick, as if he were really trying to get Rick's attention now. Rick would have to pay him a visit one of these days, he thought.

"I need to know what he is doing in my dreams. But how could he be in my dreams as well? Is this some kind of witchcraft he has bewitched me with? I will soon find out and he had better tell me the truth if he knows what's good for him. I'm usually even-tempered, but I have been through so much this past year because of these dreams. If I find out that he has been casting a spell on me all this time, I don't even know what I will do to him for payback. May God help me control myself about hurting him, and I might just hurt him bad too. And may God have mercy on him so I won't break his neck!" All these thoughts dominated his mind.

"On the other hand, I have been amazed at these adventures I have been thrown into. And the feeling of fulfillment is so overwhelming every time I helped people in need. The hopelessness, fear and pain in their eyes are usually transformed into joy with sense of security and trust that things will be okay and someone is out there to protect them." Rick positively interjected.

—   —   —   —   —   —   —

This mysterious masked man had been widely talked about now. People were aware of his existence and how he came to their rescue when they needed help. They thought of him as their hero, a handsome, mythical character who they lovingly call "The Prince" because of his extraordinary good looks and great body build. Ladies had fantasies about him. A lot of them shamelessly wanted to meet him and throw themselves at him in an act of desperation!

"What a shame! Really, this guy could only exist when I snooze. And that's how it is going to be." Rick toyed with this idea playfully. He was amused by all the adorations and flatteries he received from undisclosed admirers online.

On the other hand, men had mixed feelings about him.

Some envied his physical attributes, others looked to him for motivation and inspiration to work out, and some just plainly wanted him for themselves too!

"What a mess!" He said to himself as he let out a loud laugh.

CHAPTER 13

In California, Damon was fuming with anger caused by the unexpected emergence of the intruder on Mount Lee. He was not going to take this lightly. He had not lost any previous battle and he was not going to start now.

"No!" He brooded over angrily. "I will crush that man to pieces if it's the last thing I will ever do!"

Damon searched for any information he could find on his enemy on the internet. He found out that his opponent was quite popular. People referred to him as "The Prince" because of his good looks. Apparently, he had done considerable number of heroic services to the general public. Surprisingly, he seemed to do all these activities at night time.

"Why is that?" he thought deeply. No answer came to mind at the moment. He needed to find out more about this man.

"Anyhow, the chance of us meeting again is very possible. I should launch an earth-shattering, mind-blowing disruption so massive that he won't be able to save himself from it, much more save other people from it."

Damon meditated wickedly.

Next thing he did was to check his website, mindinterconnect.com. Browsing through his website pleased him very well. He had over two million members now and counting. The members posted information, photos, links and other pertinent facts related to their acts of violence and disturbances creating troubles and heartaches to people. The members seemed to get high talking about the crimes they had committed. They compared notes and even gave advice on how to better perform their intended offenses.

"Well done, my pawns, well done." Damon expressed his satisfaction over the progress of his website. His nerves were finally relaxed as he prepared to turn in for the night.

Tonight when Damon went to sleep, he met with Cain in his dream again. Both he and Cain devised a plan on how to defeat "The Prince" and permanently take him out of the picture. Cain could not afford to have anybody ruin his plan of creating a new world where he would be worshipped as god. He would have to act quickly to eradicate his enemy. He would need to find out more information about "The Prince".

Cain and Damon also discussed their intention to formulate an explosive devastation that would inflict severe agony and anguish on humanity. This way, people would turn away from God, thinking God had abandoned them. They would leave their faith behind and would curse God for allowing these circumstances to afflict them. They would openly defy God and His doctrines. These thoughts have absolutely gratified Cain.

"I will have my revenge on God finally." Cain viciously excogitated. He hoped that this day would come soon enough.

Damon vigorously supported Cain's propaganda without a doubt. He believed in the existence of God, but he strongly detested God. He perceived that God and religion control people with their never ending "what-to-do and what-not-to-do" rules. He hated professing Christians who look down on people who don't measure up to their "godly" standards. And he did not tolerate how God seem to favor certain people.

With Cain as god, Damon thought that everybody would have free will to do whatever they want without getting judged or punished. There wouldn't be any limits dictated by society. True freedom in all its essence would finally become a reality.

"What a glorious world it would be!" Damon rationalized internally.

Figure 6:   Prince Kilhazer Pierrum Hiertocelli

(The repugnant twin brother)

CHAPTER 14

On Saturday, Angeline was finally discharged from the hospital after 10 weeks of confinement. Rick drove her to Dayton, Ohio where her parents resided so she could stay with them temporarily until she completely recovered. Her parents had met Rick a couple of times in the past, so they were happy to see them together again. Rick stayed with Angeline until mid-afternoon then bade her goodbye. He promised to visit her again soon.

Rick made an appointment to meet with his next door neighbor, Nicholas Hahn, at four o'clock that afternoon. He rushed to get there on time. He was extremely nervous about this confrontation. He did not know how to approach Nicholas about his constant presence in his dreams, but he really wanted answers concerning all these questions surrounding this mystery. Hopefully, Nicholas would cooperate with him and would truthfully admit his involvement in all of these, if there were anything at all to admit.

He rang the door bell outside Nicholas Hahn's house. Almost immediately, Nicholas opened the door for Rick and invited him in. Once inside the house, Nicholas offered Rick something to drink but Rick refused politely. He wanted to get on with the purpose of his visit.

Nicholas pointed to the chair for Rick to sit. Then he sat on the chair directly across from him. Before Rick could open his mouth to explain the reason he requested for this meeting, Rick saw the black crystal ball carefully laid down on the center table. Nicholas purposely reached over to gather the crystal ball, holding it with both hands securely.

"Do you remember the first time you were here?" Nicholas apprehensively asked with a trembling voice.

"Yes, I do," Rick answered.

"And do you remember what you saw when you looked into this crystal ball directly, intently?" Nicholas continued asking.

Rick was not quite sure how to answer this. He did not realize Nicholas witnessed what he thought he saw inside the crystal ball. He thought it was just his imagination, the vision of a village with suffering people looking back at him as he stared at them.

"What do you mean?" Rick asked this time.

"Tell me exactly what you saw when you looked closely into the ball." Nicholas persisted.

"Here," Nicholas handed the black crystal ball to Rick.

Rick was hesitant to handle the ball, but Nicholas insisted. Once again, Rick witnessed the disappearance of what appeared to be a black veil covering the interior of the crystal ball. This time though, the people inside the ball were standing as they faced him with expectancy and hope on their faces, some were tearful, others were excited and several people were attempting to communicate with him.

Then suddenly, two people who looked like their king and queen appeared in front of his eyes. They were dressed so elegantly and elaborately, there was no mistaking that these were the rulers of the village. The king and the queen gazed back at him with such deep expressions of longing and love in their eyes. The queen had tears falling down her pale cheeks, her pain and agony apparent despite the thick wall of the crystal ball.

This show of affection made Rick wonder if he had any connection with these people he had never seen before in his life. Rick pondered about this possibility momentarily.

Rick turned to Nicholas. He was dumbfounded at this vision. He could not understand what just happened.

"What is going on here? Do I really see people tucked in inside this ball?" He held the ball in front of Nicholas to emphasize his confusion.

"Yes, what you see inside the ball is the revelation of who you really are. It's time you find out about your true identity." Nicholas slowly but clearly stated. He took the crystal ball away from Rick to ensure it would be safe from harm in case Rick reacted violently after hearing the story of his life. The story had been kept a secret from him until now, and this would change the course of his life forever.

Rick sat down. He tried to remain calm and composed as he looked directly at Nicholas, ready to listen to him.

"Before I begin, I beg of you to hear me and to have an open mind about what I have to tell you. This will not be easy for you to understand right now, but in time I believe, you will comprehend the significance of your existence as you become the person that you are meant to be. You will embrace your true identity and you will be able to accept your destiny, to be with your own people and to be the ruler of another great world." Nicholas spoke quietly.

"Over 30 years ago, you and I came to this planet, the Earth, to seek refuge and protection from our doomed planet, the Kingdom of Carbenia. We somehow got separated when we landed here, and due to the difference in time set by the distance between the two planets, we arrived here 30 years younger than our actual ages. You were but a year old when you set foot on earth and I was in my early thirties." Nicholas continued.

"I held on to the black crystal ball because it was the only way I can find you again. The ball will only reveal itself to the rightful defender, the redeemer of Kingdom Carbenia." Nicholas carried on. "Also, the crystal ball holds the future of our beloved planet."

"Carbenia is also referred to as the Black Planet because of its exterior color, black. That's why it almost appears invisible in the solar system. Little did anybody know, there was nothing black about our planet before it was maliciously conquered by your evil twin brother, Prince Kilhazer Pierrum Hiertocelli." Nicholas paused before continuing.

"Carbenia was like a paradise. It had gardens full of flowers and fruit-bearing trees, magical fairies flying all around singing and humming melodic tunes, lakes bursting with exotic fish, abundance of food and resources everywhere. It was such a pleasurable place to live in. Then your brother assembled a group of traitors, ready to defy the king in order to gain control and power of the kingdom. When they had gathered enough forces, they overthrew the rulers of the kingdom and collectively banished them into extinction inside the black crystal ball." Nicholas stopped for a moment, too many emotions starting to come back to him as he gathered himself together to go on with his narration. He briefly glanced at Rick, making sure he was paying close attention to what he was relating to him.

"I was a dear friend to the king, his confidant and his adviser. Also, I was known as the kingdom's warlock, Warlock Hahnza. I possessed great magical powers, but nothing compared to yours. You and your twin brother were given special powers and blessings by the fairies while in your mother's womb. No one predicted that our queen was carrying twins in her womb. We all assumed she had gained tremendous weight during her pregnancy. Imagine how shocked we all were when the two of you were born. But you came out first, so you were considered the firstborn son. That made your twin brother extremely jealous of you and angry at your parents. He thought the two of you should be treated equally since you were but a minute apart coming out of your mother's womb. However, the king had to designate the successor to the throne, and of course, being the firstborn son, you were given that privilege, to your brother's disgust. He has hated the king since," Nicholas shared this information with Rick passionately.

Rick was starting to feel uneasy. This incredulous story was too much to absorb. "Am I really an alien?" He thought disbelievingly. "There is no way Nicholas is telling the truth. He's delusional. I should contact social services on him so they could lock him up in a psychiatric ward. His mind has concocted this amazing fable, and it seems as though he really believes this preposterous fantasy he has created in his mind. He needs help big time!" Rick contemplated seriously.

"My dear son, I know you are having a hard time believing all this information I am telling you. Nevertheless, there is no other way to explain your dreams and my constant presence in all of them." Nicholas stated as a matter of fact, as if he had read Rick's mind.

Rick at this point had not even mentioned the purpose of

his visit with Nicholas. "How did he know about my dreams? And he just admitted his constant presence in all of my dreams too." Rick was taken aback by Nicholas' admission and his knowledge about Rick's own adventures. "Also, the way he can read my thoughts is disconcerting." Rick told himself.

"I'm sorry, Nicholas. But this story is so incredible. I mean, how could there be another planet viable of sustaining life outside the earth? And knowing that we are aliens? This is too much to take in. I am as human as anybody else in this world, and so are you. We belong to this planet, you and I, we are citizens of this world, for goodness' sake. I cannot imagine being anyone else but me, Rick Blake. I am Richard Blake. I am an American and I am proud to be an American." Rick declared distinctly.

"Yes, your conviction and dedication are qualities we are looking for in you so that you may rightfully assume your destiny," Nicholas injected.

Rick laughed sarcastically, shaking his head in disbelief while looking at Nicholas. "How could he keep interjecting this make-believe fantasy of his?" Rick deduced amusedly.

"Okay, let's say I believe you. How did you and I escape from Carbenia?" Rick asked mockingly, hating himself for behaving this way.

Nicholas was as calm and collected as ever. He responded graciously without a trace of antagonism, "When the rebels started attacking the palace, your father told me to take you and the queen into hiding. But the queen refused to leave your father's side. I forced you into hiding with me so we could formulate a plan to defend the palace and secure it from getting seized by the enemies. Alas, the enemies were strong and clever. Some evil-spirited fairies had also joined them. They defeated the king's army, captured the king and the queen, and together with all of the king's faithful supporters and followers, they were sentenced to life imprisonment. But the evil fairies suggested banishing them into extinction in the black crystal ball instead. The insurgents agreed to this punishment and it was done," Nicholas paused for a moment.

"You and I remained in hiding amidst all the commotion. After a day, I tracked down the black crystal ball inconspicuously. But someone detected that the crystal ball was missing, so a massive search was conducted throughout the entire kingdom. Innocent people were helplessly punished beyond imagination, but there was nothing we could have done. We were overwhelmed by the adversaries. Then I remembered this forbidden, disappearing wall in the deep forest that people were warned against coming in contact with. The belief was anyone who came in contact with it would disappear forever into the unknown, so people avoided it like the plague. We had no other choice, so you and I crossed that wall and we traveled into space for what felt like an eternity until we got here on earth. We came to this place for sanctuary and it has become our world as well. We have learned to love this place and to be like them in so many ways. But our true identities cannot be hidden forever. The time has come for us to assume who we really are and where we truly belong. We have a planet to save and we owe it to our own people to deliver them from the curse that has befallen them. We need to return to Carbenia and take back our planet from those evil invaders. We are ready. You are ready to take on this battle and win it. I have faith in you. You have finally arrived, your highness, the rightful successor to the throne of Kingdom Carbenia, the firstborn son of King Therouso and Queen Harnicella, my dear prince, Prince Petros Domini Hiertocelli." Nicholas announced sincerely. He gazed at Rick intently, searching his face for any signs of willingness to face the reality of his being.

Rick, on the hand, was speechless. He did not know how to respond to this. "Could this be real? This is such an elaborate story for Nicholas to have made up completely. But how do I begin to understand the complexity of this story? Am I supposed to believe this amazing allegory?" Rick analyzed silently.

"My dreams, how did I start having all these dreams about saving people? And why are you in my dreams?" Rick decided to ask Nicholas.

"You started having those dreams after you came in contact with the black crystal ball during the first time you we were here. The ball wanted the powers that you possess to come out to the surface. It made you become aware of your supernatural powers. I have been in all of your dreams to observe you, to analyze your fighting skills, your thinking ability and to evaluate your desire to help others. I have to prepare you for the battle of your life. I have to make sure that you are ready to take on that challenge." Nicholas answered without hesitation.

Rick finally realized that he started having these dreams on the night after he was here in this house for a cup of tea. That was the only time he was ever inside his neighbor's house.

"These supernatural powers I possess that you mentioned, do I only have them in my dreams?" Rick asked curiously.

"No, you have all these powers in you all the time, asleep or wide awake. But there was not a need for your powers to come out in the open, until that time when you and Angeline were attacked in the park." Nicholas clarified.

Rick remembered thinking how he fought like a professional martial arts fighter during the attack at the park that night.

"So when I dream about fighting crimes, do I get transported to the scene of the crime?" Rick inquired.

"No, that is one of your supernatural powers. You can be in two places at once. But only one of you has supernatural powers when you appear in two different places while awake. " Nicholas responded.

"Wow," was all Rick could say, impressed with his powers. He wanted so badly to believe what he heard as true. But common sense dictated otherwise.

Nicholas was silent, carefully assessing Rick's reaction to all these information he found out. "Is he going to accept his destiny? Or will he continue to ridicule this story he has heard about his own planet? Will he be willing to set his own people free or will he deny them the freedom they have lost for three decades and counting? Only time will tell if Rick will assume his responsibility to his own citizenry." Painful as it sounded, Nicholas had no choice but to accept Rick's ultimate decision.

"I will need time to process all this information you have told me. You should understand that this is a lot to take in. This is beyond my wildest imagination. I never even thought that something like this could happen to anybody here on earth, much more to me! I am the most logical person I know. And now, this is beyond logical reasoning. I just cannot begin to comprehend the complexity of this situation. And it is so hard to imagine that I am anybody else but me, Rick Blake." Rick stated acutely. He did not want to disappoint anybody, but he needed time to think alone. There was a lot at stake for the decision he had to make. And the consequences of his decision would determine the purpose of his very existence.

"Yes, I understand. Take all the time that you need. But remember, I am here to guide you from now on. Please do not hesitate to come to me if you need help in any way." Nicholas conveyed his sentiments.

"Thank you. I will keep in touch again." With this statement, Rick left to go back to his own place.

Nicholas was left to wonder what the future holds for them. He could only hope for the best.

Figure 7: King Therouso

CHAPTER 15

For the first time in over a year, Rick did not dream about fighting bad guys or helping people in need. Tonight, he had a different dream. He dreamt he was in a place so small that there was hardly any space to move in. The air supply was limited and food was non-existent. People were cramped up tightly against each other, unable to move around anywhere. They looked tired, unhappy and miserable.

Then a familiar couple he had seen somewhere came into sight. Dressed elegantly and elaborately, they slowly walked up toward him. Standing next to them, Rick noticed that they were a good looking couple despite their advancing age and haggard disposition. The king stood over six-feet tall while the queen was smaller in stature by about a foot. They both had white hair, deep blue eyes and fair skin. Both appeared slim and fragile, but authoritative and commanding.

Rick looked directly at them. He saw the undeniable expressions of deep longing and love in their eyes, the same emotions they had on their faces when he saw them before.

"My son, Petros, it has been so long since I have seen you. I have missed you so much." The Queen expressed her affection to Rick. Tears started to fall down her cheeks as she put her arms around him. She held him tightly for a while as if she never wanted to let him go.

"Petros, my son, I am so glad to see you again and to know that you are okay after all these years." King Therouso said, deeply emotional as well.

Rick was unsure how to respond to them. As far as he was concerned, these people were strangers to him. He did not feel any loving emotion toward them. He had no recollection of any fond memories he might have shared with them in the past. He just could not remember anything about them at all.

"This may sound callous and insensitive, but unfortunately, it's the whole truth. I don't know them." Rick privately rationalized.

But Rick did not want to add any further heartache to their suffering, so he kept his silence. Instead, he imagined his deceased parents showing their love and affection to him after being gone for so long. This thought comforted him and made him long for their presence even more.

Several minutes had past when the queen finally let loose of her embrace on Rick. Then she started talking again, her emotions more under control this time.

"We have been so worried about you and your brother, Kilhazer. We still cannot understand how he could have done this to us and to Carbenia. We have never treated him differently from you but he always was jealous of you growing up. Your father was following the law of the land when he designated you as the heir to the throne, being the firstborn son. It was not favoritism as he claimed it was. Neither was it because your father loved you more, because he equally loved you both. But Kilhazer won't listen to reason. His greed for power and glory has driven him to do these heinous crimes. And I don't know if this was my fault because I let him have his way all the time when he was growing up. I just did not want to see him unhappy and unloved." Queen Harnicella explained.

"Kilhazer had always been evil minded, I've observed. But for him to have done this to us was beyond anybody could ever fathom," was King Therouso's reply.

"He was consumed with hatred, jealousy and rage. His heart has turned to stone." Queen Harnicella wept bitterly.

Rick remained silent throughout this conversation. He may have been informed about what happened to Carbenia, but for the moment, he still did not connect himself to this new-found family, as well as this planet they call Carbenia. For him this was all just a dream, maybe a nightmare. He was hoping to wake up any minute now from this suffocating hallucination.

"Petros, you're awfully quiet. Are you okay, dear?" the

Queen asked.

Rick looked at her, embarrassed that he was unable to say anything to them. No words just seem to come out of his mouth.

"I'm sure this is all very confusing to you, Petros. In time, you will find yourself again. And when that happens, you know where to find us. We believe you will remember who you really are, and we will all rejoice when that time comes. Open your heart and your mind, Petros, for there you will find us, my son," the king told Rick meaningfully.

Rick could only sympathize with them. He could feel the tremendous strain and pressure they were up against. His heart went out to them.

"But could I really help them?" Rick deliberated carefully. Doubt and apprehension seriously clouded his ability to think clearly.

This was the last thing he remembered from his dream the night before. When he woke up this morning, he felt more baffled than ever before. More questions came to mind, questions only he could answer now.

Figure 8: Queen Harnicella

CHAPTER 16

The planet of Carbenia had survived over three decades of unimaginable hardship and tribulation. Gone were the days of its glory and splendor. The hills and valleys had become barren and desolate. Trees and shrubs no longer exist. Lakes and rivers had dried up. The scenic view of the skyline that was previously filled with gardens full of dazzling flowers and stately buildings that stood magnificently and aristocratically had vanished. Piles of trash, junk and debris had accumulated on the streets. Buildings had been vandalized and abandoned. Magical fairies had since disappeared from the kingdom. Carbenia had become a picture of despondency, dejection and hopelessness.

People lived in constant fear of getting killed or getting punished for no apparent reason. They cried out day and night for mercy and charity from the administration. They had been deprived of dignity, decency and morality. They're very desperate for a supernatural occurrence that would deliver them from this nightmare.

The only other option they had considered was giving

up their ghost, hoping the end would be a sweet release from this hell hole they had been thrown into.

"Life is not worth fighting for," had become the common belief they had adopted since the takeover. And nothing in their experience had proven otherwise.

The people in authority had remained deaf and blind to the plight of the citizenry. They had no compassion and sympathy toward them. They had persisted with their insensitive attitudes and abusive ways. They had no regard for the welfare of the people. And most definitely, they did not care about Carbenia and what it had turned out to be. Time will judge if the planet of Carbenia would continue to linger in this deplorable subsistence.

Figure 9:   An Insurgent in Carbenia

CHAPTER 17

Nicholas Hahn, who was also known as Warlock Hahnza, was once a great warlock in the Kingdom of Carbenia. He had spent the last 30 years on earth searching for Prince Petros since they got separated after the crossover.

To help with his search, he put up a retail store selling antiques and collectible items. Then he placed the black crystal ball on top of the front counter right beside the cash register. This way, everyone who came by the store would easily notice it given its unusual decorative appeal. His purpose was for the crystal ball to communicate itself to the legitimate liberator of Carbenia in case he happened to visit the store.

To protect the crystal ball from getting stolen or from breaking, Nicholas placed it in a specially built glass display cabinet that is secured rigidly at all corners. A big sign that read "NOT FOR SALE" was clearly posted at the bottom of the display cabinet. If the crystal ball shattered into pieces, the hope of redemption for the Kingdom of Carbenia would forever disappear into perdition. The black crystal ball held the future of

Carbenia literally.

His usual routine was to place the magical crystal ball in the sealed glass display cabinet all throughout the day while he worked. At night time after he got done at work, Nicholas would take the crystal ball out of the display cabinet into a strong box container so he could safely transport it back to his home every night. He had kept a close eye on the crystal ball all these many years.

His dedication and duty to Carbenia and its people had been his inspiration to pursue his quest to find the lost prince.

Initially upon his arrival on earth, he found himself in Oregon, a state located in the western coastal region of the United States. Through the years, he had progressively moved toward the eastern states of the country to hopefully locate the missing prince. He had been constantly moving to a different state every five years for the intended purpose.

Finally, his search was over. The black crystal ball found the prince! However, the situation remained complicated. The prince had no recollection about his true identity. He adamantly resisted assuming his destiny, and he was refusing to accept the realities of his individuality. What a dilemma!

Nicholas could only hope that time would reveal to Rick, his next door neighbor, his authentic status as the prince of Carbenia. Carbenia suffered long enough. The wait for deliverance and emancipation had long been delayed.

The people had lost their expectation for any chance of a brighter future until now. With the prince in sight, they found renewed strength and determination to pursue their fight for freedom and survival.

Nicholas would have to find a way to help Rick regain his memory. He would have to use all his skills and knowledge to hopefully bring back the lost prince of Carbenia.

Figure 10:   The Black Crystal Ball

CHAPTER 18

The Black Crystal Ball

Many years ago, the fairies in the Kingdom of Carbenia decided to get together to collaborate on a proposal to give a special gift to the King and Queen for their 60th wedding anniversary celebration. Also, the people of Carbenia wanted to commemorate the 50 years of excellent leadership and service King Therouso and Queen Harnicella had tendered to the nation.

The general public had been extremely satisfied with the way this charismatic duo had governed the land. The pair had maintained their generosity to the people. They had provided order in the kingdom through specific laws and regulations that promoted fairness, integrity and honesty when dealing with decision making process. They had inspired the people to be creative in the way they think and live to fully achieve their potential. They had blessed the people by recognizing their talents and promoting them to positions of responsibility in the kingdom.

To celebrate these milestones, the populace had decided to throw a party for the King and Queen. As part of the celebration, they would present a gift to the couple that would serve as a memento for the Kingdom of Carbenia.

"The King and the Queen have everything they could wish for--- love, health and power. What we need to give them is something of value that they will appreciate and cherish for as long as they both live." The fairies jointly agreed.

After several days of deliberation, the fairies had created this masterpiece, a black crystal ball, made of solid black diamond. It resembled the planet Carbenia in appearance and color. It was about eight inches in circumference and sat on a vase for support.

To make this gift extraordinary, the fairies collectively integrated within the crystal ball all of their individual unique magical powers. So the crystal ball was equipped to sustain life inside it indefinitely, although not comfortably. It could be used as a temporary hiding place in case of emergency. Last but not least, the fairies had designed it to be the greatest source of supernatural powers for the twin brothers, Prince Petros and Prince Kilhazer. Once the black crystal ball was destroyed, their paranormal skills would be reduced to the very minimum, tantamount to almost nothing. They would live a life similar to a common man and die a death just like a common man.

These advantages the black crystal ball had been endowed with had been kept as a secret from everybody, including the King and the Queen. Only the fairies knew about the merits of the crystal ball. They decided to keep this information to themselves to protect the sons of the King and the Queen, as well as to protect the palace from potential predators.

King Therouso and Queen Harnicella were very pleased with the present they received. They kept it on display on the wall behind the throne. It sat securely on a glass display cabinet specially designed and built for it. The King and Queen felt honored for the love and support shown by the people as evidenced by the presentation of this valuable gift. This present became their inspiration to do more for their constituents. It became the symbol for prosperity and peace of the kingdom.

Over a period of time, the fairies began fighting amongst themselves, dividing into separate groups. Some of the fairies became dissatisfied with the heads of the kingdom and rebelled against them. They joined forces with some power-hungry traitors who wanted to dethrone the King and the Queen. Eventually, they succeeded with their evil scheme.

King Therouso and Queen Harnicella had never thought that the souvenir they had treasured for a number of years would be the very thing they may have to live in for the rest of their lives. Their only hope for a future back in the Kingdom of Carbenia would rely on the willingness of the lost Prince to come to their assistance.

"This is a great day indeed! Our beloved Prince, Prince Petros, has finally come back to us!" The King's supporters inside the crystal ball stated excitedly.

"It's just a matter of time now, and he will set us all free from this den," they added.

"Yes, but unfortunately, the Prince needs time to remember his past life. Please be patient with him as he recaptures the memories of his previous existence." The King pleaded with his supporters.

"He is the only hope we have," they all agreed.

"I have faith in my son. He will not abandon us," the King assured the people firmly.

"Hopefully, he will embrace his real identity very soon. We have been in this situation for so long. It's time we fight back and recover what rightfully belongs to us," the people replied with urgency.

"Prince Petros will ultimately affirm the certainty of his past. Then he will fulfill his duty to Carbenia and to his people," the King responded confidently.

Only time could tell the fate of Carbenia and its people. That was all they had left, endless time of grief and despair.

Figure 11:   Richard Blake

CHAPTER 19

Rick was in dire need to go away for several hours to an isolated place so he could meditate on life-changing decisions.

The day was Sunday. After going to church, he decided to drive by the countryside on his way up the mountains towards West Virginia. He knew about this solitary place that would be perfect for his purpose.

After three hours of driving, he found this spot at the foot of the hills, surrounded by trees and wild flowers. Not too far ahead was a small lake that vividly reflected off the sun on its crystal clear waters. The breeze of air was cool but refreshing. The cloudless pale blue sky above stretched far and beyond what the naked eye could see. Birds sat chirping on the tree limbs. This soothing, panoramic view was exactly what he needed to clear up his mind as he mulled over the information he had received from Nicholas.

Rick learned some disturbing information about himself. He was supposed to be a prince from another planet and had a responsibility to save his people and this planet,

Carbenia. Why couldn't he remember anything about this part of his life? Granted he was only a year old when he reached the earth, according to Nicholas. But shouldn't there have been some kind of spark in him when he met his birth parents both in his dream and inside the black crystal ball? That should have triggered the bottled-up emotions he would have toward them. He felt nothing around them, no feelings of affection or any kind of attachment with them whatsoever.

What about having supernatural powers? Nicholas stated that he was equipped with these powers all of the time, whether he was asleep or wide awake. If this was true, how could he explain this phenomenon?

Then Rick fondly recalled memories about the people he considered as his parents. They had taught him Christian virtues, moral values and ethical living. He had been brought up in a Christian home where God was the center of their lives and everything else was secondary to Him.

His parents loved him dearly. He remembered how his mom used to cook his favorite food, cared for him when was sick, chased him around the house when he was young and boisterous, and read him stories at night so he could fall asleep. She was there loving him every step of the way.

His father, on the other hand, taught him "manly things." He taught him how to ride a bicycle, how to shoot a basketball, how to drive a car, how to catch fish and how to woo a girl.

Rick smiled at this thought as he remembered how his father told him how he had pursued his mother. According to his father, he carried her school bag while holding on to a stem of flower in one hand, he dropped down on one knee to ask her for a date, he serenaded her at her home, he won her parents over by helping with house chores, and so on until finally, his perseverance paid off. She had fallen madly in love with him, apparently with the same intensity as he had fallen for her. They had a wonderful garden wedding. And certainly, they had an amazing life together.

His father always said, "If you want something badly enough, you will work for it no matter what. If it continues to be elusive, keep working for it anyway. There is nothing impossible to achieve if you put your mind and heart in it. Eventually, your stars will fall right within your reach."

A hint of sadness came over him as he reminisced more nostalgic moments he shared with his deceased parents. They were looking forward to his settling down with the woman of his dreams and to their having grandchildren in the future. They used to tease him about having many children to compensate for not having siblings. Sadly, they passed away before he could fulfill their wishes.

"Mom, Dad, I will see you again someday. I love you both," Rick whispered softly.

His parents taught him everything he needed to know to

become a good man. They were honest and truthful people. If he was really adopted, why did they keep this information from him?

"Whatever happens in the future, there will always be a place in my heart for Richard Blake. He will forever be a part of me." Rick solemnly pledged.

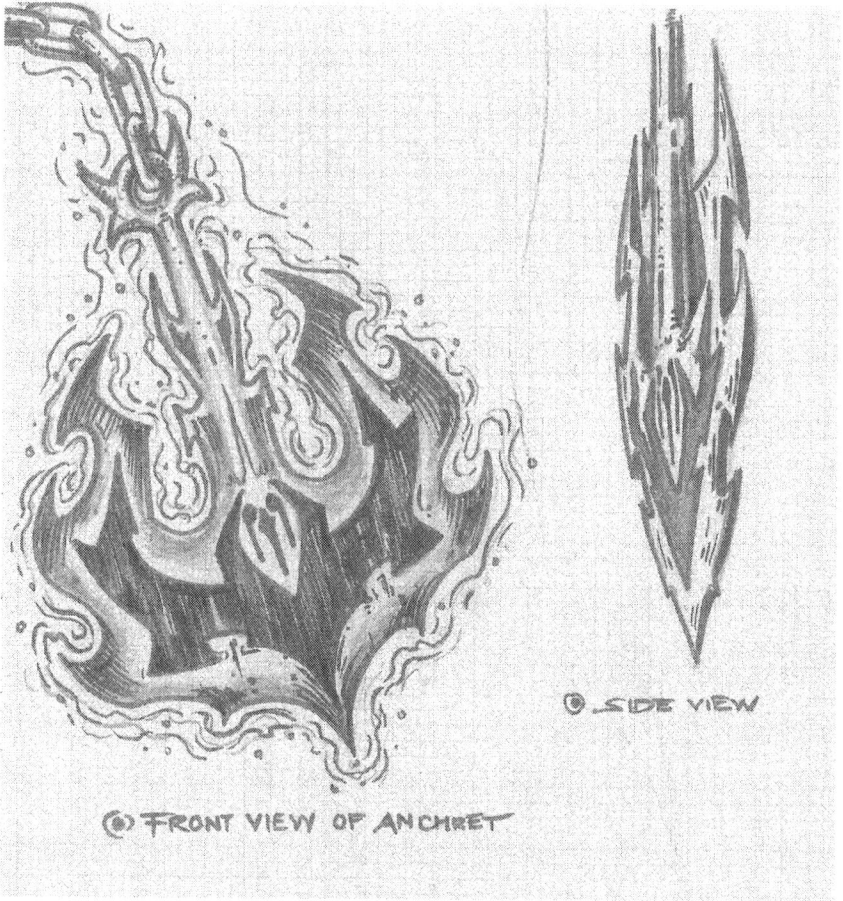

(●) FRONT VIEW OF ANCHRET

(●) SIDE VIEW

Figure 12:   The Anchret

CHAPTER 20

Damon finally started acting on the plan that he and Cain diabolically conceived. He was to cause massive earthquakes, fires, collapse of major buildings, dam failures and every other inconceivable mass destruction there would ever be in America.

The plan was for him to dig deep underneath the surface of the earth, go forward across, creating a major space gap to let the ground above cave into the hollow beneath it. He planned to start in California going all the way across to North Carolina, passing through everything above the ground including dams, buildings, mountains, roads, bridges and everything else directly above the cavernous depression.

"This will surely keep the Prince occupied as he tries to save everybody and anything above ground. Hopefully, this will be the end of him too." Damon thought wickedly.

Cain was devilishly pleased with their plan. He was definitely looking forward to people blaming God for the massive destruction about to happen. He hoped that they would turn against God and think that He abandoned them. They would curse Him for letting all these abominable devastations befall them.

"It is just a matter of time now," Cain mused with anticipation. "My victory is at hand."

Damon started excavating in San Pedro, California, a port district of the city of Los Angeles. He found a remote area along the residential community that had not been developed. Using his *Anchret* as a tool to break up concrete and the ground beneath the surface of the earth, he started digging deeper and deeper into the earth, down about 100 meters deep and creating a tunnel about 12 feet in circumference. Then he proceeded forward toward Los Angeles. Slowly, steadily, he pounded on the soil in front of him to advance to his desired destination.

Above ground, people were beginning to feel the movement of the land. Some houses situated on the path of the excavation sank, electric posts tumbled over, gas lines cracked, trees crashed down, roads were unsafe to drive on and people were scrambling for safety. Fires erupted, complicating the already chaotic state of the district of San Pedro.

Firemen and police officers were now on the scene, trying to put order into this mess. Firemen were attempting to put out the fires, but soon after one had been controlled, more houses would burst into flames. Moreover, some water pipes had been broken, resulting in limited water supply.

Police officers struggled to free people who were trapped in their homes. Some directing scared citizens to places of safety. Others managed the traffic flow to let the ambulance and fire trucks into the crisis zones.

Nobody would have guessed that this was just the beginning of a widespread turmoil. Damon aggressively continued on his conquest to generate massive destruction. He had a vision to fulfill and a mission to accomplish.

The bridge that connected the port cities of San Pedro and Terminal Island to mainland Los Angeles, the Vincent Thomas Bridge, had been compromised due to inward movement of the ground where the steel posts were once erected. This caused part of the bridge to collapse, making it more difficult to send help to the people in San Pedro.

The destruction moved more into the Los Angeles area. The inward movement of the earth's surface caused motion along the Los Angeles fault line, the Puente Hills fault, triggered a moderate earthquake in the city. This resulted in major damages to the city. Buildings toppled over, killing many people and trapping others. Bridges collapsed and freeways were damaged, causing major accidents on the roads. Power lines and gas lines were ruptured, inducing more fires to break out. Extensive property damage was everywhere. Falling structures and flying glass struck unsuspecting people as they ran for safety. The devastation continued to spread without mercy.

These catastrophic activities invaded the news channels all morning. Rick was busy at work meeting with clients in the morning, and he did not know what was happening outside his office until around lunch time. He went to the break room for lunch when he saw the news report on the television. Field reporters were giving details of the calamity that was currently in progress in California. They were also seeking the assistance of "The Prince" to help the authorities save the people in those areas. They were desperate for any kind of service or favor they could get.

Rick felt numb inside, unable to decide if he wanted to show himself at midday to thousands of people who were in desperate need of his help. He felt sick in his stomach thinking about the loss of lives if he didn't go to their rescue.

On the other hand, he would be subjecting himself to mass exposure if he came to offer his assistance. This would be his first time to be seen in public at daytime as "The Prince". This would be history in the making, something people would remember for the rest of their lives.

To make a more definitive decision, he decided to take the afternoon off from work and headed back to his house. Once inside his home, he had to make up his mind quickly.

His desire to help people in desperate need won over his need to keep his identity anonymous. Hopefully, his mask would be enough to cover up his face.

Another problem came to mind. How would he change into his costume? He did not have a costume to change into. He normally just had it on when he fought crimes in his dreams. Also, was it true that his supernatural powers actually worked whether he was awake or asleep? He would soon find out.

Now, how about that costume...? To his surprise, he was already wearing his costume. "Oh, when did I change into this?" He thought amusedly, quietly laughing at himself for still not understanding how his new-found powers really work. He began to believe that he really had supernatural capabilities.

"Now, how can I get to Los Angeles?" he thought again. He closed his eyes momentarily. Soon after, he heard loud noises in the background. He opened his eyes to find that he was already at the scene of the devastation.

The reality of this disaster shocked him beyond belief. The images shown on the television paled in comparison to the actual damages that took place in the affected areas. The affliction and torment these people were enduring far exceeded the limits of human emotions. People could be heard moaning and groaning everywhere. Some victims were screaming in pain, while others were calling for help from under the piles of shattered concrete slabs.

The whole city was in complete disorder and confusion. It was engulfed entirely with dust and ashes. Innumerable dead bodies could be seen scattered all around the city.

People frantically searched for their loved ones, hoping to find them alive and well.

Rick wasted no time. He started rescuing people from the rubble of collapsed buildings as well as those people who had been trapped inside the buildings that had remained upright. Carefully, he dug through the wreckage looking for survivors. Upon finding them, he would lift them up and carry them over to safety. Back and forth, he worked tirelessly, giving the victims his best effort.

Rick moved as fast as he could to save as many victims as possible. Time worked against him as more and more structures weakened and caused more buildings to crash down. There were many more casualties waiting for help on the damaged roads, freeways and bridges.

"This will be a very long day." Rick whispered to himself.

Police officers and firemen had been working hard to enforce control on the situation they were battling. They were extremely grateful for the help that "The Prince" afforded them. But there seemed to be no end to the devastation. In fact, it felt as if this ruin was moving more and more into the depths of Southern California.

After hours of continuous hard labor saving victims, Rick paused shortly to analyze the complexity of the situation they were involved in. He wondered why this devastation did not seem to come to a halt. It appeared as if the path of it was threading on a straight line through the entirety of Southern California. Like something, or someone, was purposely inducing this unthinkable depredation. But what was it, or who was it? Who could be so evil enough to inflict so much pain and misery on people?

Then like a flash bulb, the image of that beastly warrior with whom he had fought on Mount Lee came back to his memory.

"Could it be possible that he has something to do with all this?" Rick tossed this idea in the back of his mind.

"There is no way anybody other than myself has such supernatural strength and power to bring about this kind of destruction here on earth. Or is there?" He questioned himself silently.

He proceeded in providing services to the needy. However, this thought about the possible involvement of that madman persisted in his mind, and he made up his mind to investigate this hypothesis. If proven right about his intuition, then this nightmare was not going to end soon.

Rick began to look closely for any sign that might lead him to the root of this mess. He followed the trail where this problem had begun. It led him back all the way to San Pedro, California.

In San Pedro, amidst the pile of clay and soil on the ground, he found a hole so deep he could not see what was inside it without actually going into it. He plunged into the hole and followed the tunnel in front of him. So much debris had already blocked some parts of the tunnel caused by the structures that fell into it. Rick thought about getting himself out of the hole, and instead, he followed the path of destruction toward Los Angeles.

Once there, he decided to create a hole in the ground as well. He was hoping to meet or see what or who was responsible for this atrocity. Using his body as a deep-hole boring machine, he twirled around like a cyclone, penetrating the ground surface as he went down deep beneath the earth. He was hoping to come across the tunnel made by this unknown criminal.

Finally, he came face to face with the perpetrator. Yes, he was right about his intuition. Once again, he met this muscular warrior who was not too thrilled to see him either.

Damon turned around to face Rick squarely. His hatred toward Rick was evident with every step he took to get closer to his opponent.

Poised with the *Anchret* on his right arm, Damon stood fiercely as he braced himself to attack this intruder. He lifted his right arm, steadily swaying the *Anchret* in front of him as he started moving toward Rick. Closing the distance between them, Damon recklessly swung the *Anchret* in full force, intending to bash his enemy with it. His passionate desire to exterminate this meddler had become top priority for him.

To keep from being punched in the limited space of the tunnel, Rick acted fast. He quickly moved to the wall beside him, climbed up on it like a spider as swiftly as he could, and crawled along the curvature of the tunnel, maintaining the alignment of the spot where he was cornered, landing safely on the opposite side of the wall. Rick avoided getting thumped by the *Anchret* for now. He was able to outpace Damon's speed while whirling the *Anchret* around and unyieldingly pursued Rick with it.

Rick decided to take this fight out into the open field above ground to get Damon out of the excavation site. This would prevent him from continuing to dig beneath the earth and avert the spread of the calamity and misery. Luckily, Damon followed Rick out of the tunnel when the latter escaped out.

On the ground above, Damon growled out loud like a wild animal to show his aggression and anger. He moved into successive actions, relentlessly pursuing Rick. He kept swinging his *Anchret* every possible way as he advanced again and again toward Rick.

Rick went on the defensive over and over. He would reach across to try to grab the *Anchret* from Damon's grasp, but the madman proved to be equally strong. He attempted to sneak up behind Damon to no avail either. Damon was pumped up with pure adrenalin and was moving as powerful and as fast as Rick could manage. He seemed to be on equal footing with Rick.

On and on, this battle dragged on. Both Rick and Damon persevered to outperform the other, pounding on one another as the opportunity presented.

After several attempts, Rick caught the *Anchret* by the chain close to its head. He tugged it as hard as he could while Damon cleaved to it. They contended to wrestle on through this tug of war, hoping to bring the weaker challenger down to his knees.

Neither one of them was budging, so Rick devised a plan quickly. With all his might and strength while holding on to the *Anchret,* he started moving his arms above his head going around on a circular motion, taking Damon along for the ride. Faster and faster, he continued his swinging motion until finally, he let go of his hold on the *Anchret,* causing Damon to fly about in the air across the distant area where the rubble of collapsed buildings remained.

Rick thought he finally scored a major point on Damon, only to realize that the move did not cripple his opponent at all. Damon readily came bouncing back ready to strike again.

"Whew, we've been going at this all night long. Something's gotta give, someone's gotta go," Rick thought exasperatedly. He was feeling exhausted and vulnerable as the attacks kept coming at him. He was running out of options. He felt like something really drastic had to happen in order to defeat this lunatic.

"But what could it be?" The question lingered in Rick's mind.

Meanwhile, too many bystanders were now watching their rumble. Field reporters were also on the scene

111

capturing the highlights of the nasty fight. People were stupefied at this supernatural encounter between two masked men with unusual strength and skills. It was almost like watching a science fiction movie. The difference was that they were actually witnessing an occurrence so unbelievably real unfolding right in front of their very eyes.

"What an incredible experience indeed!" People thought while they watched in amazement.

Nicholas Hahn was also present and watching this showdown. He was interested in finding out how it would be resolved. The duel had been going on for some time, but neither seemed to be winning. Not one of the two wanted to concede defeat. He was actually amazed that someone not from Carbenia could possess this much power and challenge Rick.

"Not from this planet anyway," Nicholas was intrigued. "Could there be many more like him?"

Looking around, Nicholas noticed a certain man watching this combat intently as well. Thinking back, Nicholas had seen this man at several locations. The man stood out even when he was trying to remain inconspicuous. His manner of dressing was different, granted some people had weird senses of style anyway. Regardless, this figure spoke mystery. He was dressed as a shepherd tending to his flocks, wearing an-off white tunic like one of those men in the older times or like some character from the Bible. His attire was complete with matching sandals and a cane in one hand.

Then Nicholas saw that this man was clutching onto something with his other arm. He was holding on to it tightly, protectively, as if his life depended on it. Out of curiosity, Nicholas deliberately moved closer to this man, keeping a nonchalant attitude and pretending that he just happened to stand alongside him like the rest of the spectators.

Upon close scrutiny of the object in question, Nicholas came to the realization that this man was holding on to an object that looked like a replica of the anchor-like device Rick's ardent foe had been using as a power tool.

"Could there be a correlation?" Nicholas deliberated.

He had to think quickly, clearly and logically. This discovery could have been the solution to this intricate problem all along. He had to take a chance at this. He devised a plan to snatch the object out of the man's grasp without serious repercussions. He did not know the extent of this man's ability and powers, to say the least. But if he were able to organize a catastrophic crisis of this magnitude and launched a monster warrior into existence, then this man should not be taken lightly. He must have been a man with great powers as well.

Nicholas contemplated on a course of action to carry out to take possession of the anchor-like device. Being a warlock himself had major advantages. He had tricks in place that hopefully would work in his favor, but he had to carefully decide which trick to use for this kind of predicament.

"It's time for action," Nicholas convinced himself.

Taking a bold step toward the mysterious man, Nicholas seized the stone replica of the *Anchret* away from the man's protective clasp and disappeared from view.

Cain was caught unaware. He did not anticipate that anything like this could happen. He did not even see whoever it was that took the stony replica away from him. He had taken the *Anchret* out of Damon's display cabinet for safekeeping while the disaster was in progress. He thought it was best to bring it with him until this pandemonium had settled down. Alas, things had taken an unforeseeable turn for the worse! He lost the precious item right in front of his eyes! How stupid could that be? He began to panic. He was trembling violently with rage.

"This is not happening. I must find it. I can't lose the *Anchret*. It is the heart and soul of this entire operation. The success of this movement relies on it. How could I have been so reckless?"Cain blamed himself. His full attention had been focused on the battle between "The Prince" and Damon. He should have paid close attention to the people around him too.

Who would have thought somebody would grab the *Anchret* away from him? Did they have the slightest idea about what that object could do? Or did someone just extract it from him for fun? Or maybe so they could make money out of it? He was furious at whoever took the stony figurine. He needed to concentrate now so he could recover the valuable missing apparatus.

Cain focused his attention to the view in front of him. He was equipped with a special power for concentration. He could ignore any distraction that would possibly cloud his search for anything. He could see through people's clothing in search of the object he wanted to find, even from a distance.

Like looking for a needle in a haystack, he swept his glance across the sea of people who crowded the streets. One by one, he slowly looked them over for any sign of the missing jewel.

Then a breakthrough came, he spotted a man carrying something inside his coat. He wasted no time in approaching this man, only to find out he made a mistake. The man did not have the *Anchret* on him.

Cain continued on his quest to find the *Anchret*. He followed any possible lead that might take him to the figurine. He was hoping that the spirits contained within the *Anchret* would show their wrath at the thief and punish him for stealing.

Meanwhile, Nicholas remained invisible to the naked eye. He headed toward Rick to pass him this heavy piece of stone he had stolen. He noticed that the figurine was getting heavier by the minute. Looking down on it, he noticed several pairs of burning eyes staring at him with displeasure. The image was disconcerting, but he kept moving toward Rick.

After several minutes had passed, Nicholas' trick of invisibility wore out. He proceeded to walk even faster to arrive at his target location. He sensed that he was not walking alone anymore though. A throng of evil spirits swarmed around him. They were furious at him, pulling at his arms so he would loosen his hold on the *Anchret,* scratching him everywhere causing cuts, lacerations, tears, scrapes, gashes and bruises on his skin. Nevertheless, Nicholas endured all the pain he felt and grasped tighter to the *Anchret.* He was not going to let go, even if this would kill him.

To make matters worse, the wicked spirits started adding more trouble to the already distressed city of Los Angeles. They were hurting people on purpose. They facilitated more structures to collapse, trap and kill bystanders. They caused more fires to break out in various locations. To say that they were mad as hell was an understatement to describe their reaction to this intrusion.

Nicholas hurried along, not caring that he was in so much pain from the injuries he had sustained. His mind was focused on delivering the package to Rick as soon as possible. He knew now more than ever that what was in his hands was very valuable. It could be the solution they needed to end all of these problems they were fighting against.

Cain recognized the spirits living inside the *Anchret.* He

was very pleased to see them out in the open and aggravating people's miserable conditions. Also, their presence would finally lead him to the punk who had the audacity to steal from him.

"He will pay greatly, I swear," was all Cain could think about once he caught up with this bandit.

From a distance, Cain could finally identify the culprit. There was no denying who the offender was this time. The spirits flocked around him like moths to a flame. They gathered around him, chasing him wherever he went. Cain walked faster to catch up with him.

Nicholas had finally reached his destination. He could see Rick actively wrangling with the psychopath. Nicholas needed to get Rick's attention immediately.

Rick sensed within himself that Nicholas was in the vicinity. He looked around calculatedly, expecting to see Nicholas. Sure enough, he saw Nicholas waving at him. Something else caught his interest. Nicholas was pointing to an object he was holding tightly with his other hand. Rick concentrated on the image being pointed to him. It must have been something extremely significant for Nicholas to interrupt him while he was engaged in this physical encounter.

Rick suddenly realized the object in question was the exact replica of the anchor-like device his opponent had been using all along. With this thought in mind, he rushed to Nicholas and accepted the stony replica. Nicholas also gave him an instruction to destroy the *Anchret* beyond repair to forever eliminate his enemy. This however, depended on the presumption that this precious stone was the source of power for Damon's supernatural abilities. It was something worth finding out though, they both decided.

Cain finally caught up with Nicholas. Rick took possession of the stony replica then flew up in the air. He was trying to decide how to effectively obliterate the *Anchret* forever without the possibility of it getting put back together.

Cain was so angry at Rick for taking the *Anchret* away and flying up into the sky. He was more than irate at Nicholas for stealing the precious stone from him.

He pointed his cane at Nicholas, letting out an electric power surge to electrify him and sending Nicholas across the street. But Cain was not done with his revenge. He intended to finish off the man responsible for taking the *Anchret* away from him. He would kill him.

Nicholas was so beaten up that he could hardly breathe or move a muscle. But he had to pull another trick to save his life hopefully. He managed to pull the invisibility trick once more so he could not be seen by his assailant.

Cain went over to where he thought Nicholas had landed, but he could not find Nicholas there. There was no sign of him anywhere.

"Hopefully, I have hurt him enough to cripple him for the

rest of his life." Cain muttered to himself, too furious that his enemy had escaped his wrath.

"I will hunt him down for the rest of his life if it's the last thing I ever do." Cain swore in anger.

Meanwhile, Rick kept flying higher and higher up into the sky, going way beyond the earth's boundary and into the solar atmosphere. Some of the spirits that dwelled within the *Anchret* followed him vigorously, determined to take back the *Anchret*.

Rick formed a more definitive decision about the permanent destruction of the much sought-after stone figurine. He would toss it straight up into the sun.

With this in mind, he headed toward the sun. He wanted to move as close as he could get to the sun, not minding the enveloping heat and blinding brightness of the sun's reflection and its atmospheric pressures.

Convinced that he had reached the point at which he could cast the stone figurine into the sun for its ultimate destruction, Rick prepared himself for the task at hand. Striking a pose with the *Anchret* in his right hand, Rick raised his right arm as he gathered his momentum, then with all of his strength and energy, he threw the stone figurine directly into the sun. Not long after, he heard the *Anchret* exploding into the sun.

The spirits who chased Rick disappeared into thin air as soon as the *Anchret* was blown up. The same thing happened to the spirits left behind on earth.

Rick was confident that the stony figurine had been totally annihilated. He left to go back to earth and finish off the turmoil that had beset America. He hoped that what he accomplished in outer space had helped to ease the situation on earth.

As he headed back to earth, he noticed a black planet partly concealed behind the planet Jupiter, situated almost between the planets Jupiter and Saturn. It was a much smaller planet than the rest of the planets in the solar system.

"But it's definitely a planet. Could that be Carbenia?" Rick speculated.

He would soon find out. Right now, he needed to get back to earth as soon as he could. A more appropriate time would soon be allotted to recover the lost planet of Carbenia.

"First things first," Rick considered thoughtfully as he hurried back to earth.

Figure 13:   Warlock Hahnza

CHAPTER 21

Rick was back in Los Angeles. He started locating his fiery archenemy in order to settle their dispute once and for all. To his utter surprise, he found Damon sprawled out on the ground, barely breathing, with his anchor-like device shattered to pieces beyond repair. He appeared to have shrunk in size too. His bulging muscles were not as pronounced as they once were. And he was definitely not as tall as he used to be.

With this pathetic sight, Rick concluded that the fight was over between him and the shrunken warrior. He turned his attention to finding Nicholas, who was left behind to face the wrath of these attackers.

"Where could he be hiding? I hope he is okay," Rick prayed earnestly.

As if on cue, Nicholas appeared in full view. He was hurt badly but he would survive this ordeal. He had a bigger challenge to face in the near future, the conquest for the Kingdom of Carbenia.

Rick was concerned about Nicholas's welfare after seeing

his pitiful condition. But Nicholas assured Rick that he would be fine after a few stitches. He advised Rick to focus on the task at hand. He had more pressing issues upon which to dwell and more problems about which to worry.

Rick assisted Nicholas into the ambulance for medical treatment. Then Nicholas was transferred to the hospital for further medical intervention.

Rick had resumed rendering relief and support to the authorities in an attempt to bring about some order and peace for the devastated city.

People applauded him as soon as he emerged back into view. There was a momentary pause as people cheered and shouted over and over, "The Prince! The Prince! Long live The Prince!"

Rick was overwhelmed with emotion as he waved to the people. He was no longer concerned about being seen in public. His main objective was to perform and complete the mission he had set out to do.

Dawn started to break over the horizon, signifying the beginning of another day. Hundreds of people gathered together hand in hand as they persisted in giving aid to everyone in distress. Millions of people across the country and even the world prayed zealously to God for mercy and deliverance of the people in California. People who were backsliders turned to God in prayer. More and more people amazingly started praying to God.

The affected cities had suffered tremendously, but hope was in sight. Despite the massive destruction and the heavy casualties, people were determined to rebuild their lives as they look forward to a future filled with optimism and possibilities.

CHAPTER 22

Damon had been taken to the hospital for treatment of his wounds and broken bones. Afterward, he had been transferred to a mental institution for severe psychological breakdown consistent with Schizophrenia, the mental disorder he had been diagnosed with. He was being sedated around the clock to control his outbursts and aggression. He was also placed on a five-point restraint to prevent him from hurting anyone.

On the other hand, Cain had fled the scene of the catastrophe, his head bowed down in shameful defeat. He had hoped that people would hate God for bringing such calamity into their lives. He was almost certain that the general public would lose their faith in God after suffering so much misery that ruined their lives. But to his dismay, the opposite came to be. More people sought God in their time of need.

The enigma of human emotions remained a mystery to Cain. It surpassed his understanding of why finite mortals seek the divinity of the infinite God Almighty despite the torment and torture they had experienced. God had given people freedom to choose and act as they please.

But people have chosen to come back to God's protection and guidance time and time again.

"Why is that?" Cain asked himself quietly, immensely perplexed over this puzzle.

"Cain, Cain, why do you always challenge me? When will you ever learn the lesson of life? Good always triumphs over evil, just as life always prevails over death," God reminded Cain.

"I will never be subjugated under your dominion. I will prove to you one day that the very people you have created to worship you will turn their backs on you. They will hate you," Cain replied, uncontrolled rage evident in his trembling demeanor.

"Have it your way, Cain. I will be here waiting for you. Come to me and I will give you rest, my child," God urged Cain patiently.

"Never," was Cain's firm response.

Without a choice, Cain accepted his failure this time. He promised to come back with a vengeance at another time. Until then, he was left to be a restless wanderer on the earth once again.

CHAPTER 23

Once order had been restored to the stricken areas in California, Rick decided he could start planning his next move in his life.

He came to visit Angeline at her parents' home. He made up his mind to tell Angeline that he would not be coming back for a very long time.

Angeline was in tears, and so was Rick. He learned to love her beyond life itself, but his duty to his own planet came first and foremost now. He had a destiny to fulfill and that did not include her. Although in the future, if he made it back to earth, he hoped to have a life with her permanently.

But time and distance would not be on their side. The possibility existed that he would never see her again. And this was the greatest sacrifice of all, a sacrifice that was necessary to accomplish his obligation and allegiance to the Kingdom of Carbenia.

"Was it something I did? I know things have not been the same since the attack, but I am getting better. Soon I will be my old self again and everything will be just the way they were. Could you hang in there a little bit longer?" Angeline asked Rick. She already knew in her heart that she had lost Rick.

"I'm afraid I can't. I am going on a journey and I sincerely don't know when I'm coming back. It's not fair for me to tell you to wait for me because I don't know if I will be able to make it back. Live your life to the fullest even without me. Just remember, you are by far the best thing that has ever happened to me. I love you, Angeline. You will always be in my heart." Rick responded passionately, pain and heartache evident in his eyes.

Rick could not explain to Angeline why he was leaving. It was a complicated matter that's best kept a secret forever.

"I don't know what's going on with you, but please don't shut me out of your life. You know I'm here for you, don't you? I'm always going to be here for you when you need me. You can count on that. You can trust me, Rick," Angeline stated, trying to convince Rick to open up to her.

"This is something I have to do alone. I'm so sorry, Angeline." Rick responded sadly.

Angeline sobbed in despair. She was so heartbroken. She was losing the love of her life and there was nothing she could do.

The hurt in Angeline's eyes was too much to bear, but again, he had no choice. He finally said goodbye to her.

He left without looking back because of the intensity of emotions he was feeling in his heart. He cried silently as he drove away.

"I will never forget you, Rick. I will love you forever." Angeline said softly to herself as she watched Rick disappear from her life for good.

CHAPTER 24

Rick went to pay his grandmother a visit at the nursing home in Toledo. Grandma Josie was unusually talkative today, although she still did not recognize her visitor. She kept on babbling about her baby doll and how she would like them to have matching clothes to wear.

On her bedside table were picture frames of photos Rick had not paid attention to in the past. He carefully scanned each of the photos now, a tinge of pain and sadness sweeping over him as he looked at pictures of the people he thought were his parents all along. They had loved him beyond a shadow of a doubt, and he loved them in return. He had a wonderful life growing up with them. And he would forever be grateful for the love and support they had given him.

Grandma Josie moved her wheelchair to stay beside Rick as he stood looking at the photos. She reached across and handed him the Bible that was also on the table. He accepted the Book graciously, smiled at her warmly, and was about to put the Book back into the bedside table when it accidentally fell to the floor. The Bible contained loose papers and envelopes tucked neatly into the pages inside. Rick began to gather all the scattered papers together when he noticed an envelope with his name clearly written on it. He picked it up and noticed that it was still sealed tight.

"How could there be a letter addressed to me in Grandma's possession?" Rick was confused. He studied the envelope closely, and from the looks of it, the letter had been kept there for a long time. The white envelope had turned yellow, but the writing on it clearly stated his name.

"It's for me, so I guess I can open it...?" he said out loud without expecting his grandmother to answer him back.

He opened the letter carefully. It was from his adopted mother. She had written this letter about 15 years ago, on May 24, 1998 to be exact, on his 16th birthday. It read....

My dear son Richard,

Before I start with this letter, I would like to tell you that I love you so much. Your father and I are very fortunate to have you in our lives. You are the greatest blessing God has ever given us. And we would not trade you for anything in this whole world. Please remember that as you read this letter.

Today, you turned 16. This is a milestone for you as you begin your walk into manhood. You have been a very good son to us and we are so proud of you. I hope you will have the wisdom to understand the purpose of this letter. I don't have the heart to tell you this in person, neither does your father. That's why I decided to write this letter to you, hoping that when you read this, you will not treat us any differently from how you used to.

Richard, we are not your biological parents. We found you crying as you sat by a tree in the wooden area beside our property. You were probably just a year old then. We took you in, put some clothes on you because you were naked, fed you and took care of you. Then we posted your photos everywhere to hopefully locate your parents. But nobody came to claim you, so we kept you and decided to adopt you as our very own son.

We have not told you this before because we would like to think that God has purposely sent you our way to give meaning to our lives. You have brought us so much joy that the thought of you being taken away from us now is something we might not be able to handle. But deep in our hearts, we know that you have the right to know the truth. But this truth will not change the fact that we love you dearly, and we will always love you as our very own son.

Please forgive us for keeping this a secret from you.

Your loving mom,

Elaine

Rick was speechless. This was the revelation he had been searching for in order to assume his destiny. He may have had doubts about his true identity even after finding out about his supernatural powers, but now, he had finally found his confirmation.

Rick kissed his grandma goodbye as he hurried to leave. He had someplace else to go.

Figure 14:   The Lost Prince of Carbenia

CHAPTER 25

At the cemetery, Rick paid respect to his adopted parents. Strong emotions welled up inside him. His love for them had not diminished even after finding out the truth about his identity. They would forever remain as the parents he had always known here on earth, and he was eternally grateful to them.

"I have become the man you have raised me to be, and I know you will be proud of me as I become the man that I am supposed to be. I am Prince Petros Domini Hiertocelli, the successor to the throne of Kingdom Carbenia. I am the son of King Therouso and Queen Harnicella, and I have a responsibility to my people. I have to set them free and take back Kingdom Carbenia from the intruders who have brutally invaded the planet I belonged to. As God is my witness, I will avenge my people. So help me God."

With this conviction, Rick officially acknowledged his true identity.

Made in the USA
Charleston, SC
11 October 2013